UNOFFICIAL GUIDE

The BIG Book of

APEX

LEGENDS

The ULTIMATE GUIDE
to dominate the arena

©2019 CHOUETTE PUBLISHING (1987) INC.
Text: Michael Davis
Illustrations: Electronic Arts Inc.

Cover background: Shutterstock
All screenshots for criticism and review. Apex Legends™ & © 2019 Electronic Arts Inc.

CrackBoom! Books is an imprint of Chouette Publishing (1987) INC.

Chouette Publishing would like to thank the Government of Canada and SODEC for their financial support.

Bibliothèque et Archives nationales du Québec and Library and Archives Canada cataloguing in publication

Title: The big book of Apex Legends: the ultimate guide to dominate the arena/ text, Michael Davis; illustrations, Electronic Arts Inc.

Names: Davis, Michael, 1981- author. | Electronic Arts (Firm), illustrator.

Identifiers: Canadiana 20190029315 | ISBN 9782898021367

Subjects: LCSH: Apex Legends (Video game) Juvenile literature | LCSH: Computer war games—Handbooks, manuals, etc.—Juvenile literature.

Classification: LCC GV1469.35.A65 D38 2019 | DDC j794.8/5—dc23

Legal deposit – Bibliothèque et Archives nationales du Québec, 2019.
Legal deposit – Library and Archives Canada, 2019.

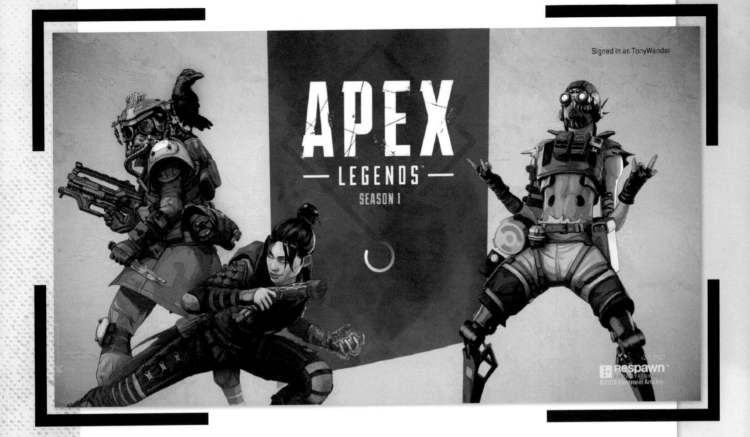

BASICS

This section covers the basics of Apex Legends, from controls and heads-up display (HUD) to drop strategy and locations. Shall we?

WHAT IS APEX LEGENDS?

Apex Legends is a first-person shooter in the genre of battle royale (last player-slash-team standing wins). Up to twenty teams of three players each compete in a shared map location called King's Canyon. The game is set in the Titanfall game universe, and takes place thirty years after the events of Titanfall 2.

Each player chooses a specific Legend with distinct special abilities. As that Legend, they try to gain a combat edge by collecting weapons, attachments, ammo, gear, and items. The game presents a level playing field for all: Legends can be customized cosmetically, but their combat abilities can't be upgraded.

Working together in their squads, players attempt to eliminate other teams to win the match. Players can be revived during the course of play, though at some risk to their teammates.

Play is broken up into eight rounds. After each round, the "circle" surrounding the active play area shrinks, forcing players closer together. Straying outside the play area will drain the health of a player, eventually killing them. Typically a team will win the game within four rounds or fewer.

> Multiple Platforms

Apex Legends is available to play (for free!) on three different platforms. PC, PlayStation 4, and Xbox One. Familiarize yourself with the nuances of your platform, because it may affect your control scheme and graphics fidelity.

> Multiple Skills to Master

It is not enough to simply aim well in Apex Legends. Players must master skills and acquire knowledge to ensure victory. These include:

- Knowledge of the map and points of interest
- Movement
- Combat
- Knowledge of available weapons and equipment
- Special abilities of their Legend
- Team communication

Each of these skills is examined in the following chapters, with specific strategies and tips on how to improve them.

> No Friendly Fire

You can't be shot or harmed by your teammates in Apex Legends, so don't worry about accidentally killing a teammate. But offending them with a stray bullet and losing a friend? That's a different matter.

> Controls

Controls in Apex Legends can—and should—be customized to suit your playing style. You've probably spent a lot of time building up muscle memory for a certain layout and recreating that layout will help you improve in the game more quickly.

> Display

Apex Legends offers players a substantial and sometimes overwhelming amount of information via the heads-up display (HUD). Here is what you need to keep an eye on.

> Top left: Map

The map is extremely useful, indicating the location of hot zones (large blue circles), supply drops (small blue circles), respawn beacons (small green dots), and supply ships (ship symbol).

> Top right:
Squads Remaining

This part of the screen gives you information about the teams that remain in the game. Pay attention to how many other squads are in play; this will give you an idea of what stage of the match you're in.

> Bottom left:
Player Health and Teammate Health

Obviously you want to monitor your current status, up to 100 health and 100 shields. (Don't forget to maintain it at 200 at all times if you have the items for it). But also keep an eye on how your teammates are doing, especially if you are a Legend with healing capabilities, like Lifeline.

> Bottom right:
Current weapon/ammunition

As discussed, you'll usually want to reload whenever you get a chance. But this readout can also be useful for weapons, like the Mastiff shotgun, that have a fixed amount of ammo.

LEGENDS

Playing as a Legend is arguably the most distinctive aspect of Apex Legends. It's even in the title! Each legendary character has a unique look, plus three special abilities offering an advantage in combat, movement, and team survival. Some abilities are more team oriented; others favor stealth, agility, or simply raw power. So while Apex Legends is already a formidable game for its graphics and fast-paced combat, the legendary characters allow players to customize their experience for their specific play style.

> Abilities

Each legendary character has three unique abilities falling into the following categories:

> Passive

These abilities are always "on," meaning that you don't need to activate them. Examples: Gibraltar's automatic shield popping up whenever he aims, Octane's steady trickle of health recovery, or Wraith's whisper ability that warns of nearby enemies and traps.

> Tactical

This ability needs to be activated by the player and takes a short time to recharge afterward. An example: Bangalore's smoke-grenade launcher, which creates a wall of vision-obscuring smoke.

> Ultimate

It is another ability that is activated by the player, but it takes much longer to recharge than the tactical ability. To reflect the high cooldown cost, the ability is usually pretty awesome. An example: Lifeline's ability to call in a care package containing valuable high-tier equipment for her team.

> Hitboxes

Besides the character's capacities, be very careful of the hitbox that matches their general size (though Respawn has indicated that they may tweak hitbox dimensions in future patches to the game). For now, know that bigger, bulkier characters like Gibraltar are easier targets, and smaller characters such as Wraith are harder to hit.

WRAITH   LIFELINE   WATTSON   OCTANE   BLOODHOUND   MIRAGE   BANGALORE   PATHFINDER   CAUSTIC   GILBRALTAR

THE LEGENDS

The following is a breakdown of the available legendary characters as of Apex Legends Season 1 and Season 2, along with notes on their special abilities and play style, as well as comments on the various Legends they complement.

All Legends are not created equal, and some are considered better than others. For this reason we have listed them from (arguably) the most useful to the least. Play style will dictate whether you agree with our assessment, though, so make sure to experiment and find the best fit for you.

LIFELINE

Combat Medic

Summary

Straight up, Lifeline is probably the most useful legendary character in the game—a must-have on any Apex Legends team, even if she's not your flashiest option. What makes her so valuable isn't her offensive abilities; instead, it's the support she provides to her entire squad. She helps everyone survive, and even can supply critical loot for her teammates.

Players using Lifeline should always be keeping an eye on squad health; sometimes they should even sacrifice engaging in combat to play a supporting role instead. So if you love running in with guns blazing, perhaps this Legend is not for you.

Note that as of Season 2, Lifeline—like Wraith and Pathfinder—takes an additional 5% damage from every source (explosion, melee etc.) to compensate for her smaller hitbox.

Works Well with

Pretty much everyone. Lifeline is widely regarded the two first seasons MVP (Most Valuable Player), thanks to her highly useful healing abilities and the fact that she can use her ultimate ability to call in high-tier loot for her teammates on a regular basis.

Abilities

Don't expect to lead the charge with Lifeline's robust support abilities. Instead she'll support team members from behind the scenes, maintaining them in peak fighting form.

Passive Ability – Combat Medic

When Lifeline uses healing items, her passive ability reduces the healing period by 25% compared to other Legends, which is a major advantage in such a fast-paced game. She also deploys a handy shield wall while reviving teammates, which protects her and her teammates during this vulnerable process. Not bad for a passive ability!

Tactical Ability – Drone of Compassion (DOC)

This excellent tactical ability offers a trickle of healing to nearby teammates over time. It's super useful to lay down when your team is defending a fixed position: It continually tops up everyone's health, providing a massive advantage that can counter damage the squad may experience in the midst of a firefight.

OVERVIEW

HOW IS APEX LEGENDS DIFFERENT FROM OTHER BATTLE ROYALE GAMES?

At first glance, Apex Legends may seem like only a slight variation on the battle-royale format we've all come to know and love, but on closer look, you'll discover many features that set it apart from other games in the genre, such as Fortnite.

> Faster Combat

Game play in Apex Legends is much more frantic than in Fortnite for several reasons. First, the map is smaller—small enough, in fact, that you can cross it from one side to the other during the course of a single match. This means more players per square foot—and also more fighting. Second, mandatory team play forces fighters to stay vigilant and in motion: All of your hard-earned combat skills amount to nothing if you're outnumbered three to one. Finally, player avatars are more agile: They can climb higher, slide faster, and traverse the map more nimbly. This feature makes holding a superior tactical position more difficult, and rewards players who stay on the move.

> Shorter Rounds

Because Apex Legends has fewer players and a smaller map than Fortnite does, games finish faster—typically, within fifteen and twenty-five minutes. Many players consider this an advantage: In the same time frame, you can play more games of Apex Legends than of Fortnite. You may also experience less frustration if you're eliminated at the last minute in Apex Legends, because you've invested less time getting there!

> Less Camping

A viable strategy in Fortnite is to camp in a safe spot and take out foes from afar with a sniper rifle. Apex Legends discourages that tactic. Because players can move from point to point much more quickly, they can more easily confront rivals, like snipers, who occupy the same spot for too long.

Also, staying in place is a poor team strategy. You're much more useful to your squad when you're on the move—collecting valuable loot, providing backup on the ground, and pinging useful locations.

Finally, Apex does not allow players to lie flat on the ground—only to crouch. It's time to pratice your squats!

All of these factors combine to make sniping a losing proposition.

> Less Silly

Gone are the fun dance moves of Fortnite and its playful special items, like the Boombox, which debilitated enemy players by making them groove to a sweet beat.

Apex isn't a super gritty game, but its emphasis on combat and its sci-fi vibe are calculated to reach *a more mature demographic* than Fortnite's.

> No Vehicles

Unlike Fortnite, Apex Legends features no vehicles. You probably won't miss them, as the game offers plenty of other methods of transportation, like balloons and zip lines (more on these later). In addition, the smaller map means you won't be traversing long distances.

> Leave Your Pickaxe at Home. And Your Hammer, Too, While You're At It!

Harvesting building materials is a major component of Fortnite, separating the amateurs from the pros. Players construct their own cover, gain a height advantage, and even trap other players with building strategies. No matter how good you are at combat, if your building and harvesting skills in Fortnite are poor, you're guaranteed to lose.

But there's no build mechanic in Apex Legends. The focus is on combat, with the innovations discussed above. This development can be a good or a bad thing, depending on how good your building skills are. You may find it a relief to focus on stalking other players.

> Mandatory Teams

While Fortnite does offer a team-match option, its most popular style of game play is "every man for himself." Apex Legends mandates three-player teams—no more, no less—for every match.

If you're not online with two other friends, the game will randomly assign players to fill out your team. (Which can be problematic: A complementary mix of Legends is essential to a team's success.) Teamwork rests at the heart of Apex Legends game strategy, as we'll discover in these pages.

CONTENTS

INTRODUCTION

When Electronic Arts announced the development of its new battle royale, Apex Legends, fans of games like Player Unknown's Battlegrounds (PUBG) and Fortnite were pretty excited. For this release, EA promised a fresh take on the genre.

Apex Legends came through on that promise, offering faster, more agile, and more nuanced combats thanks to an enhanced Source, the engine used in Titanfall 2. Another innovation was the ability to play as "legends" characters possessing different passive and active special abilities. The last innovation was the game's emphasis on teamwork, via a robust "ping" communication system.

The result? Apex Legends is quickly becoming the must-play battle royale. As an early player, you're in a great position to get comfortable with all the game's nuances ahead of the pack and level up your skills. This guide covers everything you need to know about Apex Legends— all the tips and tricks you need to get a leg up on the competition.

But enough preamble. Let's jump into the epic world of Apex Legends!

Ultimate Ability - Care Package

Lifeline's packages are a gift that keeps giving—literally! This ability summons down a care package for the squad that's filled with valuable loot.

While the contents of Lifeline's care package skew a little toward defensive and healing items, they'll also include an occasional piece of offensive gear. Note that this particular ultimate ability takes more time to recharge than that of any other legendary character, so don't forget to use it early and wisely.

Be aware that calling in a care package will alert other teams to your location, so it might be strategically smart NOT to use this ability late in the game if you wish to keep your position secret. That said, you can also use the noise of the care-package delivery to decoy or ambush opponents who come to investigate.

WRAITH
Interdimensional Skinisher

Summary

Wraith is one of the most popular characters in these early days of Apex Legends, and her play style favors aggressive combat. It's no surprise: She has a good mix of useful abilities, and—frankly—a pretty awesome look.

Note that while Wraith currently has the smallest hitbox in the game, Respawn has addressed this tactical advantage: In Season 2, Wraith takes an additional 5% in across-the-board damage.

Works Well with

Gibraltar. When he activates his group shield, Wraith can use her ultimate ability to create a dimensional rift inside the shield, then sneak out using her tactical ability (very brief invulnerability to damage and near-invisibility) to distance herself from the battle. Then she can create the other entrance to her rift, creating a handy escape route. When Gibraltar's shield finally goes down, the entire team can retreat to safety in the blink of an eye!

Abilities

Wraith's abilities are all about mobility. Whether whisking herself or the entire team out of harm's way with her ultimate ability, she is a valuable teammate for any squad.

Passive Ability - Voices from the Void

This is a very useful reconnaissance ability that gives a sound prompt when an enemy is aiming at you or your team. It won't tell you where the enemy is, but it will tell you that you're about to come under attack, which is extremely valuable information, particularly if the team is busy healing. A button prompt allows you to pass the word to your team instantly. Voices from the Void also gives an alert when traps are nearby.

Tactical Ability - Into the Void

This is a great ability for escaping a sticky situation, as it makes Wraith almost invisible (except for a translucent blue trail), nullifies enemy damage, and gives her a 20% speed boost. Used properly, this is a get-out-of-jail-free card for Wraith, allowing her to find a safe spot to heal up. Be aware that the duration of this ability is quite short, only few seconds, so don't waste time once it is activated.

Ultimate Ability - Dimensional Rift

This ability can be a bit confusing to use and requires some planning, but really comes in handy. When she activates her ultimate ability, Wraith drops a dimensional rift wherever she happens to be standing. She receives a speed boost she can use to move quickly to another location and place a second rift before the timer runs out. Now any player (including members of other teams) can pass through the rift and fast-travel between the two locations. These portals last for about 60 seconds. So watch out!

This ability makes Wraith very useful as a scout. For example, as teammates are looting an area, she can drop a rift, then use her tactical ability to move invisibly to the next area. When teammates are finished looting, they can catch up with her by following in her footsteps through her dimensional rift.

The fact that enemies can also use Wraith's portals is of tactical value. Since the portals are commonly used for retreating, many teams will charge through them hoping to catch a fleeing Wraith. Imagine their surprise when the rest of the squad is waiting on the other side to ambush them.

GIBRALTAR
Shielded Fortress

Summary

Gibraltar is a legendary character commonly referred to as a "tank." Big, bulky, and powerful, Gibraltar has special abilities that protect himself and his team from harm. His ultimate ability provides great offensive cover.

While Gibraltar's hitbox is the biggest in the game (making him easier to hit), he doesn't move any slower than the other legendary characters do. He only appears to: It's an illusion caused by the slower movement animation and his height from the ground.

Gibraltar's greatest strength is the ability to make a whole lot of noise and thereby distract enemy teams. But he can use his passive ability to shield himself while simultaneously opening fire—which lends itself well to a simple strategy in which he pins down enemies with sniper fire from the high ground while his teammates execute a flanking maneuver.

Don't expect to lead the team in kills with this legendary character, but if you miss the long-range combat that is largely discouraged by Apex Legends's play style, Gibraltar is unquestionably the guy for you.

Works Well with

Wraith (see above).

Abilities

Passive Ability: Gun Shield + 15% Damage Reduction

Gibraltar's always-on ability takes effect whenever he uses his weapon sights to aim. This activates a shield that blocks nearly all incoming fire. It bears mentioning that a superbly aimed shot can still get through, so don't get overconfident.

Gibraltar is given a 15% damage reduction across the board to compensate for having the game's biggest hitbox.

Tactical Ability: Dome of Protection

Gibraltar's tactical ability involves a simple dome shield that stays active for 18 seconds, repelling enemy fire. It also blocks outgoing attacks from inside the dome, so stay near the edges of the dome, strategically dipping in and out to launch offensive tactics against enemies.

Ultimate Ability: Defensive Bombardment

Defensive bombardment may sound like a contradiction, but that's how this ability is used best—to create chaos so your team can regroup or retreat. Don't expect to make many kills with it—sound cues give the enemy lots of advance warning that you've activated this ability—but it's great for buying the team some time to create separation from the battle and seek out security.

BLOODHOUND

Technological Tracker

Summary

The mysterious Bloodhound is a very useful legendary character whose abilities allow them to gain a greatly enhanced understanding of the battlefield. As their name suggests, they have a specific talent for running enemies to ground.

They are especially valuable in close quarters, like buildings, but they are also skilled in tracking down injured opponents in order to finish them off. If you're playing as Bloodhound, be careful not to wander too far from your group, though, because they aren't powerful enough to operate solo for long periods.

Bloodhound's tactical ability—which lets them sense traps and enemies through walls—makes them absolutely indispensable for squads in the early game. They can provide valuable intelligence that will help your team clear buildings or pass through potential ambush points. Use pings frequently with this character, as their superior awareness of enemy movement is a major advantage.

Near the end of a match, when so much combat occurs inside buildings, Bloodhound's tactical and ultimate abilities are extremely advantageous. Knowing what's on the other side of a door can mean the difference between a victory and a loss.

Works Well with

Bloodhound's ultimate ability, which allows them to see enemies through smoke and gas, complements the talents of Legends like Bangalore and Caustic, whose own special abilities enable them to impair the vision of friend and foe alike. You can use Bangalore and one of these two Legends to create a scenario like this one:

Everyone is struggling to see through the murk of smoke and gas. Everyone but Bloodhound. While the rest of the players stagger around blindly, they activate their Beast of the Hunt ultimate ability and systematically takes down enemies as if it's as clear as day.

Abilities

Passive Ability - Tracker

By default, Bloodhound can see tracks left behind by enemies. This ability has limited usefulness, though, because the map is small: You can find tracks literally everywhere. But it does come in handy from time to time—for instance, when an enemy with a shattered shield has retreated and you want to hunt them down and finish them off.

Tactical Ability - Eye of the Allfather

The Eye of the Allfather allows you to see hidden enemies, clues, and traps through walls and structures—very handy if your squad is looking to loot a building and wants to make sure it's safe to do so.

Ultimate Ability - Beast of the Hunt

This is a great ability which highlights enemies so they're easier to see (even through smoke and gas) and speeds up your movement as well.

BANGALORE

Professional Soldier

Summary

Probably the most well-rounded legendary character in Apex Legends, Bangalore is extremely proficient at regular combat, with a nice mix of offensive and defensive abilities. New players could choose far worse legendary characters to cut their teeth on. Bangalore's abilities are straightforward and uncomplicated.

Because Bangalore is built for a more progressive play style, expect to be leading a lot of attacks with this character. She works with great effectiveness in close combat, so make sure you prioritize a good shotgun for her. Be ready to push in on opponents using her passive-ability speed boost.

Bangalore also excels in a support role, as her smoke launcher and Rolling Thunder abilities can be used to create time and space in which your team can regroup, heal, and reload.

Works Well with

Bloodhound. As discussed earlier, Bangalore's smoke grenades pair well with Bloodhound's ultimate ability that enables him to see through smoke.

Gibraltar. Bangalore's close-quarters combat prowess synergizes well with Gibraltar's gifts for long-range combat. And they both have airstrike abilities which, when deployed at the same time, can seriously clear out an area.

Abilities

Passive Ability – Double Time

Bangalore moves 30% faster when she is under attack—and Apex Legends being Apex Legends, that means she moves faster pretty much all the time. Note that "under attack" doesn't necessarily mean taking damage. Her passive ability is activated anytime bullets are fired in her vicinity. Use this speed to close gaps quickly if you're in a long-range battle with your opponent. Bring the fight to their front door and spare no one!

Tactical Ability – Smoke Launcher

The smoke launcher is a double-edged sword, as it impairs the view of both enemies and teammates. This ability is very useful in providing cover during a retreat, though, as well as in causing generalized chaos on the battlefield. You can't hit what you can't see (not without a considerable amount of luck).

The smoke launcher has a charge of three rounds, each of which lasts 15 seconds before dissipating, so you can use this ability a couple of times in a row before the mandatory recharge kicks in. Consider prioritizing the optical attachment called Digital Threat (see the *Attachments* section for more information) so that you can make out your enemies through your own smoke.

Ultimate Ability – Rolling Thunder

This is an artillery bombardment that creates a wall of destruction that moves slowly across the landscape. Unfortunately, this weapon is fairly easy for enemies to dodge, because it gives the enemy plenty of warning, and you need to be quite close to throw the beacon which ignites the barrage.

Rolling Thunder is at its most useful when used defensively, to create a deadly wall between you and opponents that grants your team some breathing room to heal or retreat.

Used offensively, Rolling Thunder can dislodge enemies from cover and send them running, and thus make them more vulnerable to attack from your teammates. Be aware that Rolling Thunder can also concuss you and your squad, so always communicate with one another before activating it.

CAUSTIC
Toxic Trapper

Summary

Caustic is a legendary character that must be unlocked—to the tune of 12,000 Legend Tokens or 750 Apex Coins. He's worth every penny though: His powerful close-quarter combat skills and tactical abilities are an asset to any squad.

This legendary character is at his best indoors, in closed spaces, where his gas traps can block corridors and pin down opponents. If you can survive to the late stages of a match, where combat often ends up taking place in buildings, Caustic is a guy who can get you across the finish line.

But Caustic is also an asset in the early game, where his abilities can start damaging enemies before he even picks up a weapon. For instance, if your squad targets the supply ship, he'll give you a slight offensive advantage against the other as-yet-unarmed squads heading there.

Works Well with

Bloodhound. Caustic uses gas to blind his enemies, and Bloodhound's ultimate ability allows him to see through it. Together, they can absolutely punish a squad caught in the disorienting fumes.

Abilities

Passive Ability - Nox Vision + 15% Damage Reduction

Caustic can easily see enemies that are inside his gas clouds, which is a huge tactical advantage. For this reason, you should make use of his tactical ability as often as you can. In Season 1, his passive ability gave him a 10% damage reduction to offset the disadvantage of his outsized hitbox—which is second only to Gibraltar's in targetable surface area. In Season 2, this damage reduction has been increased to 15%.

Tactical Ability - Nox Gas Trap

Caustic's traps look like big propane tanks. When shot or triggered, they release a cloud of toxic gas that causes damage and highlights enemies so Caustic can easily see and target them. The canisters can also be used as light cover until/if they are destroyed. Remember: Caustic's gas hides him from enemies, but it doesn't actually shield him. He can still be hit with a lucky shot.

Ultimate Ability - Nox Gas Grenade

Caustic's ultimate ability behaves like a thrown grenade, bathing a large area in his Nox gas. This can be very useful if you're setting up a defensive perimeter, as he will easily be able to identify anyone entering the gas cloud and can warn teammates that an attack is imminent.

WATTSON

Holographic Trickster

Summary

A new legendary character in Season 2 of Apex Legends, Natalie "Wattson" Paquette brings some very interesting play dynamics to the game. Her abilities are decidedly mechanical, which makes sense: As her backstory has it, she's the daughter of the lead electrical engineer of Apex Games.

Wattson will strongly appeal to players who like to game out their strategy in advance. Her abilities may lack the flash of Octane's or Mirage's, but used with forethought she can be a powerful asset, a teammate who becomes only more valuable as the game goes on and the play area becomes smaller.

When playing as Wattson, you'll want to stay in constant communication with teammates. For one thing, the protection from attacks offered by her Interception Pylons cuts both ways—destroying the grenades of foe and friend alike. That's an important thing to know about in the heat of battle, when you're trying to use your limited supplies of ordnance in the most effective and economical way. Rather than stockpiling grenades when you're playing as Wattson, you'll want to seek out the Ultimate Accelerants that combine so powerfully with her passive ability.

Work Well With

Since Wattson excels at controlling and defending small areas, she teams up exceptionally well with Lifeline: Her Perimeter Security ability can provide Lifeline with the time and protection she needs to call in air drops or heal teammates. Note that hiding a Perimeter fence behind one of Lifeline's indestructible air drops is a good strategy. An unsuspecting enemy who stumbles into the fence will suffer all kinds of damage before he can figure out what's happened to him.

Caustic is another good teammate for Wattson: She's good at creating enclosed areas, corralling enemies into them, and defending them. He's good at punishing foes inside such areas using his gas traps.

Finally, Pathfinder can also be a pretty good complement for Wattson. By drawing on his ability to determine the future location of the shrinking ring, he can help her plan the locations of her static defensible positions for the endgame well in advance.

Abilities

Passive Ability – Spark of Genius

This ability increases the Ultimate Accelerant's effect fivefold: Instead of a standard 20% recharge, it provides a full 100% charge instantaneously. Additionally, when Wattson is in close proximity to one of her Interception Pylons, she receives a boost in the recharge time of her tactical ability. Note that the proximity should be within a grenade's throw distance.

In Season 1 of Apex Legends, the teammate who could do the most with an Ultimate Accelerant was Lifeline. In Season 2, that teammate may be Wattson, thanks to her great passive abilities.

Tactical Ability – Perimeter Security

This is one of the coolest and most exciting abilities of this new character: Wattson can lay down up to twelve "nodes" and use them in any combination to create an electric fence. Perimeter Security thus gives Wattson the ability to assist the group in hunkering down and defending a position.

Wattson's electric fences may appear to function in the same way Gibraltar's protective dome does—i.e., as protection—but they have some distinct and important advantages. Three of them, to be exact: When passing through the field of Wattson's electric fence, an enemy will:

1) take damage;

2) become slower;

3) trigger an alarm that will be received by you and your teammates.

The fence posts can be destroyed by enemy fire, so try to conceal or disguise their location by deploying them behind features of the landscape or objects like doors or boxes. The electric fences will shut down briefly when Wattson or a teammate passes through them.

Note that Wattson can lay down only three of her twelve nodes at one time. Before adding more, she requires a cooldown of twenty-one seconds. At the end of a given mission or operation, she should retrieve the nodes: Gathering them up again will recharge her tactical ability.

Ultimate Ability - Interception Pylon

This is a useful device that Wattson can strategically place in the location of her choosing. It projects an electrical field which provides several advantages:

1) it will destroy any grenades that pass through a large radius—including the grenades of teammates. Important note: It will also repel the special attacks of both Bangalore and Gibraltar no matter if you are playing them as teammates or as enemies.

2) the pylon will regenerate shields for everyone in the vicinity.

3) standing close to a pylon will accelerate the recharge time of Wattson's tactical ability.

Note that enemy players can destroy an Interception Pylon, so try to set yours up in a fairly sheltered location, or one that's at least somewhat shielded from the enemy's angle of attack.

Wattson can hold three Interception Pylons at a time.

PATHFINDER
Forward Scout

Summary

Pathfinder is a highly mobile (and charming!) legendary character with the ability to move quickly around the map, thanks to his zip-line and grappling-hook abilities.

Pathfinder is at his best when acting as a scout for the team, taking the high ground to get a good idea of what lies ahead. It's incumbent on him to transmit this vital information to his teammates, so if you're going to play as this character, you should be fairly competent in your communication skills, both pinging and verbal.

Generally, though, Pathfinder turns out to be one of the less useful Legends. His abilities don't really complement anyone else's; the increased mobility he offers, with his zip-line and grappling skills, doesn't compare favorably with (for instance) the pure speed of other characters.

But his passive ability (to gain intelligence about the positioning of the closing circle) and his tactical ability (to create zip lines) can be of value. And honestly, he's worth playing with every once in a while just for his fun and bright dialogue.

In the early game, Pathfinder's zip-line gun is valuable for ferrying your group from one looting location to another, and his ability to gain the high ground quickly can be beneficial to a team engaged in a flanking maneuver. Just don't get so carried away with his mobility that you find yourself separated from your squad when there's trouble.

Note that as of Season 2, Pathfinder (like Lifeline and Wraith) takes a 5% damage increase across the board to compensate for his smaller hitbox.

Works Well with

Pathfinder doesn't synergize especially well with any other character, though his zip-line ability can enhance the mobility of players like Gibraltar or Mirage, that don't have speed-up abilities. A team that already has Wraith or Bangalore can probably pass on taking Pathfinder, as his strengths are redundant next to theirs. Ok, he can be also useful to Wattson to determine the future location of the shrinking rings thanks to his insider knowledge.

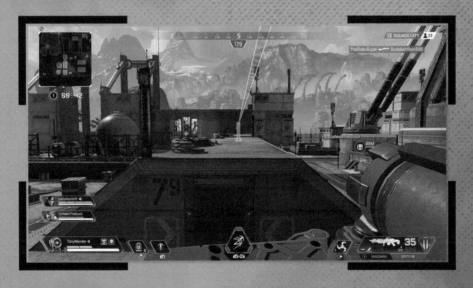

Abilities

Passive Ability – Insider Knowledge

Pathfinder can seek out survey beacons and scan them to reveal the closing ring's next location. That's useful for long-term planning, but it frankly pales in comparison to the passive abilities of most of the other legendary characters.

Tactical Ability - Grappling Hook

This is an extremely fun ability which allows Pathfinder to gain the high ground quickly. If you practice, you'll find you can determine the direction of your grapple by the direction you're facing when you retract the grapple line. Skilled players can use the grappling hook to arc around enemies or even pop up over obstacles. Pathfinder is a character that loves, loves, loves the lack of fall damage in Apex Legends.

Incidentally, you should know that you can also use the grapple line in the same way Mortal Kombat's Scorpion does—to pull enemies toward you. Get over here!

Ultimate Ability - Zip Line Gun

Pathfinder can create a zip line that the entire team can use—for instance, to quickly traverse the map, or to reposition themselves behind and/or above enemies. We're not saying that this ability isn't quite useful for mobility purposes, but again, compared to the awesome power of other legendary characters' ultimate abilities, it's not that compelling.

OCTANE
High-Speed Daredevil

Summary

Octane was the first character added to Apex Legends after the initial launch. He's a fast Legend optimized for reckless behavior and aggressive combat. To unlock him will set you back 12,000 Apex Coins or 750 Legends Tokens.

Octane is a good choice if independent play is your thing. He has the highly enviable ability to speed up on demand, and he's a good choice if you like being in the thick of the action. That said, don't be surprised if you find yourself, as Octane, constantly in need of being revived by the other members of your squad.

Works Well with

Octane is a lone wolf, which is to say that he doesn't synergize so well with the other Legends. Avoid combining him in a squad with Pathfinder, as his ultimate ability to create a launch pad overlaps with Pathfinder's zip-line ability.

Abilities

Passive Ability – Swift Mend

This is a really solid passive ability, as it automatically restores Octane's health. Combined with his speedy tactical ability, it will make it possible for you to plunge into battle and do some serious damage, then get out and lick your wounds.

Tactical Ability – Stim

After activating this tactical ability, Octane moves 30% faster for six seconds—which is a massive benefit in combat. In many Apex Legends skirmishes, six seconds will be all you need to win a firefight. That said, this ability costs 10 health to use, so bear that in mind when you're activating it. If you're on your last legs, it could end up doing you in instead of helping you out.

Ultimate Ability – Launch Pad

Octane can drop a jump pad that will catapult teammates through the air. It's a tool that can be handy in beating a retreat, getting inside a closing circle quickly, or pushing up on an enemy squad that is optimized for long range and has you pinned down. In the fast-moving universe of Apex Legends, the element of surprise can be a lethal weapon in and of itself.

MIRAGE
Holographic Trickster

Summary

This Legend is available for purchase from the in-game store at a price of 12,000 Legend Tokens or 750 Apex Coins.

Mirage is among the least useful of the legendary characters, because his abilities depend heavily on trickery, and everybody knows it. If someone's already expecting you to pull a fast one, it's that much harder to fool them. Mirage's abilities can be deadly in the hands of an experienced player, though: When deployed intelligently, they can create enough confusion in battle to turn the tide.

Works Well with

Generally, Mirage doesn't synergize well with other players. He does have slight synergy with Bangalore and Caustic, who can use their smoke and gas clouds to give him cover when he activates his special abilities.

Abilities

Passive Ability - Encore!

When Mirage is knocked down, he creates a holographic decoy Mirage and the real, injured Mirage becomes temporarily "invisible." In practice, this invisibility is fairly underwhelming—a faint but distinct outline that will be visible to other players, particularly experienced ones. Anyone who's even remotely familiar with Mirage's passive ability will not be fooled by this bait-and-switch.

Tactical Ability - Psyche Out

Mirage's holographic decoy mimics the behavior of an active player—and not very convincingly, to be perfectly frank: If the hologram happens to encounter a wall, it will simply stop dead in its tracks and like a zombie, remains in place. Be careful, because many enemy players will immediately recognize what you're up to if they witness you activating this ability. It's a special effect that can't stand on its own, basically; you need additional special effects to pull it off. So try working in cooperation with players like Bangalore or Caustic, whose smoke and gas abilities can be used to conceal you during the decoy-activation process.

Psyche Out can also be useful for inducing hidden enemies to give away their position: In the heat of battle, when they see an enemy run out into the open, they may not recognize him as a decoy, so they may not be able to resist shooting at him.

The decoy can also play a helpful role during the drop: Mirage can cast a hologram and dispatch it in another direction to lure other teams into wasting their time and ammunition.

Ultimate Ability – Vanishing Act

This ability creates a small army of holographic Mirage decoys and also cloaks himself (be careful though because his outline can be faintly seen). The Mirages in this mini army are significantly more useful than the passive-ability Mirage who gets dumbfounded when he runs into walls: In fact, should the enemy get too close to them, the ultimate-ability Mirages will actually open fire. They can come in handy in a bad situation, because they can buy you time to escape. Even so, an ultimate ability that simply buys you time to escape isn't really that exciting.

DROP

In this section we will take a closer look at the game's first moments, when teams choose their landing locations and drop from the sky. Picking a good landing spot is critical; it can significantly benefit (or weaken) your team later on...

As of Season 1, Apex Legends has a relatively small map called King's Canyon that features seventeen named areas. The game randomizes loot among locations that are mostly fixed, with guaranteed higher-tier loot available through hot zones, supply ships, and supply drops.

No location is the loot-bonanza equivalent of Fortnite's Tilted Towers, but here's a good general rule: The more buildings in an area, the more loot it offers. Let's look at some higher-tier looting areas that are attractive drop destinations:

> Hot Zones

A hot zone appears at the beginning of every match, represented on the map by a blue circle. In this area, players are more likely to find valuable loot, including high-tier armor and weapons equipped with useful attachments. Expect hot zones to be high-risk areas for combat, as other players will surely be drawn to them.

Hot zones appear randomly at locations you can expect other teams to prioritize from the drop ship. But if a hot zone is distant from the drop ship's flight path, fewer teams will make their way to it. That's why you should maximize your distance-covering ability during the drop by executing the "wave drop," which is described in greater detail later in this section.

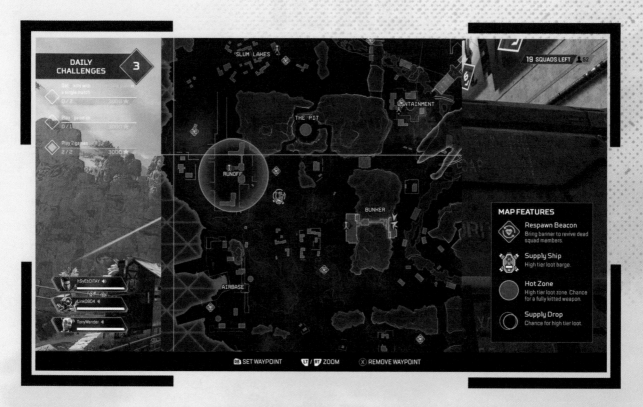

> The Supply Ship

The supply ship is a looting bonanza, offering the best initial loot in a match. Marked on the map with an icon of a ship, it follows a set path to its final destination, where it deploys zip lines to allow grounded players to reach its high-tier loot offerings.

Sometimes the supply ship will drift close enough to your drop ship that you can board it midflight. You'll probably be facing off against two or more other squads, but if you manage to survive, you and your teammates will walk away tricked out with some decent weapons and equipment. Nothing ventured, nothing gained!

> High-Density Building Areas

Outside of hot zones and the supply ship, no specific area guarantees rarer loot than the rest, but high-density areas will have better odds, because they'll hold more loot in general.

> Named Locations

While no specific location is notably superior to any other, some do offer particular advantages. Generally speaking, locations at the edges of the map are less popular, though this is always a function of the route of the drop ship. Of course, if the drop ship travels directly above an area that's typically isolated, more teams than usual will choose it as a drop location.

> Thunderdome

Despite its name, Thunderdome, in the farthest southwest area of the map, is a relatively peaceful spot to start the game. Few players tend to land or loot in this small area, so it's a viable and safe place for your team to begin equipping itself. Plus it's just northeast of Skull Town, which is a great second location.

> Relay

Tucked away at the far northeastern edge of the map, this is another great landing spot if your team includes newer players who aren't immediately ready for a firefight. It's conveniently situated close to a great second location called Artillery, which has many loot-laden buildings and hangars. At Relay, your squad can quietly outfit itself with the basics, then proceed to Artillery for solid upgrades and a bit of fighting.

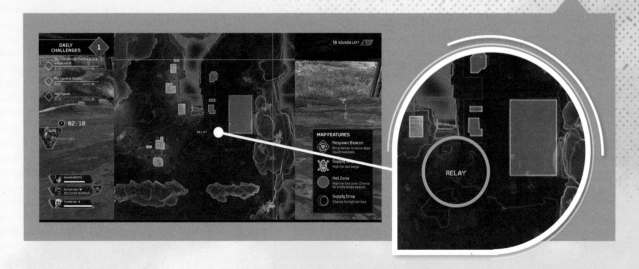

Hydro Dam

The Hydro Dam is popular for its loot and its proximity to other useful areas. As a landing zone, it's recommended for more experienced players: The price of its loot is a certain amount of combat. Snipers, take note: This area also has some great camping spots.

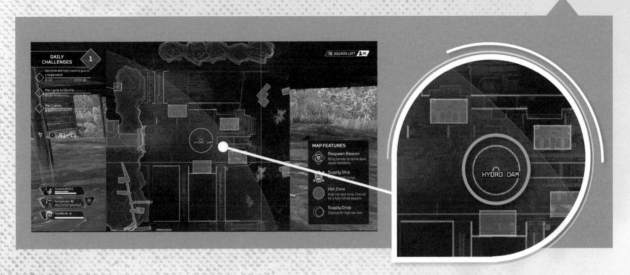

Bunker

Another relatively central location, Bunker will expose you to some combat, but it's a paradise for players that prefer submachines guns (SMG) and shotgun weapons. The bunker is basically one long hallway with rooms to either side. It's a simple loot location to memorize, and the close-quarters fighting may be an advantage to players who prefer that style. The downside: Bunker is a little light on loot. Luckily, there's more outside!

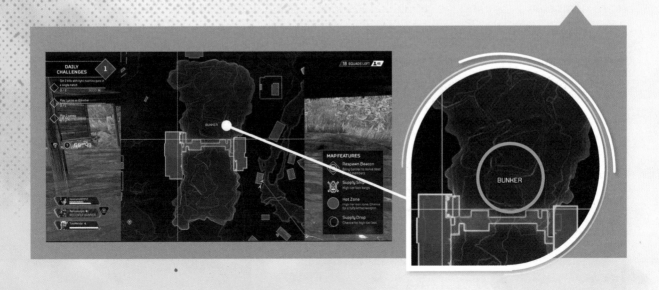

> Market

In Apex Legends, the harder a place is to get to, the less popular it will be. But some of the more central locations, like Market, are definitely worth a look, if you're willing to fight for your supper.

Market, which is roughly as popular as Hydro Dam, offers a large indoor market which is great for close-quarters combat. After you gather loot in the main area, consider popping by the massive cave next door for even more. The most useful Legend in this location is arguably Caustic, as he can hide his gas traps in the nooks and crannies of many rooms.

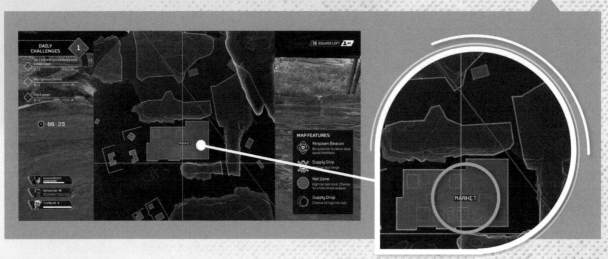

> Containment

Even if it was unnamed, this area was already a popular landing spot in Season 1. It's still a great place to start the game, and you can expect Containment to be even busier and even more competitive. Starting the game there is ideal for the numerous loot and decent cover. Basically, a nice trade-off between dangerous and having lots of good loot.

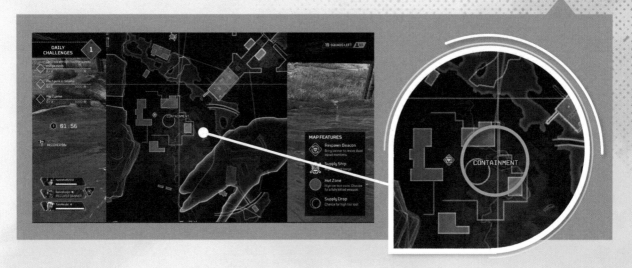

> The Cage

This may be the most tantalizing area added to the map for Season 2. The developers of Apex Legends describe The Cage as a "behemoth that was created by an organization called the Mercenary Syndicate in order to draw competitors to its supplies like moths to a flame."

Located near the center of the map, northwest of Hydro Dam, The Cage is a six-story building that's absolutely jam-packed with loot. As with the Containment area, you can anticipate heated competition here from enemy players. They (and—unfortunately—you) are the moths to the flame of the abundant rewards this location offers. Just make sure it's them, and not you, who goes up in smoke.

> Shattered Forest

There were hints of them in Season 1—mysterious, massive creatures known as Leviathans existing outside the playable range of the map. In Season 2, these formidable beasts reside roughly in the center of the map, and nest in the location unofficially known as Shattered Forest. (Observant players will note that the Leviathans' migration from open water down the river has caused significant damage to surrounding areas.) Vegetation in this area is now substantially lusher than it was in Season 1. Note that Shattered Forest is still unnamed on the map.

You can't fight Leviathans—they're way too freaking big—but you can sometimes find valuable loot when they lift their enormous feet. Move quickly, though! If you get caught between a Leviathan's foot and the ground, you'll be squashed like a bug.

Shattered Forest is also where the winged reptiles known as the Flyers seem to nest. Since they always carry death boxes that can be shot down, this is a great area to find them.

GENERAL DROP TIPS

We talk about landing and strategic locations but you still have to master your drops! Indeed, the drop drop is a vitally important part of Apex Legends. In these early moments, good drop protocol and skills will give your team a valuable speed advantage.

> The Jumpmaster

During each drop, the player on the team who takes the longest time to pick his Legend is designated as the Jumpmaster. If for some reason a player doesn't actually make a selection, the Jumpmaster will be the player who takes second-longest. The Jumpmaster controls when, and in what direction, the team ejects from the drop ship. The game assumes that by not actively picking a Legend, the inactive teammate may be away from the game for some reason. Of course, Jumpmasters can also relinquish their role in the game and pass it onto someone else.

During the landing, you should generally stick with your Jumpmaster: You don't want to end up too far away from your teammates. After landing, you can all head to different buildings and nearby areas to loot up more efficiently.

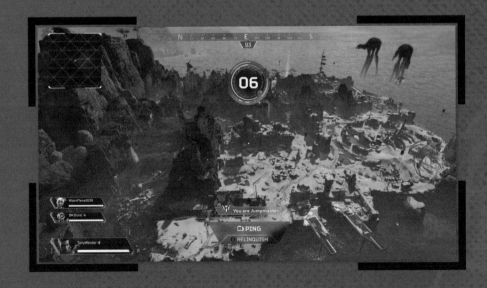

> The Wave Drop

While you're dropping, pay attention to the extremely useful gauges on the left and right sides of the screen. The left-hand gauge provides information about your squad's airspeed, and the right-hand gauge shows your altitude.

During a standard drop, the Jumpmaster is always pushing forward, toward the intended destination, by pointing with his directional controls. Simply doing this will give you a range of about 700 meters. But you're a better player than that!

As you move toward your intended landing point, pay attention to your airspeed. Once it falls below 130 or 140, execute a dive by aiming your camera toward the ground. This will make your avatar accelerate; your airspeed will jump within just a couple of seconds. Once your airspeed reaches 145 to 150, level out and glide toward your destination. Whenever your speed drops below 130, dive again.

Practice this technique to maximize your jump distance. Eventually, you and your squad should be able to access looting locations that are simply out of reach for other players.

A properly executed wave drop will give you an upper limit of approximately 1,400 meters of additional distance. Always ping your intended destination to determine how far away it is.

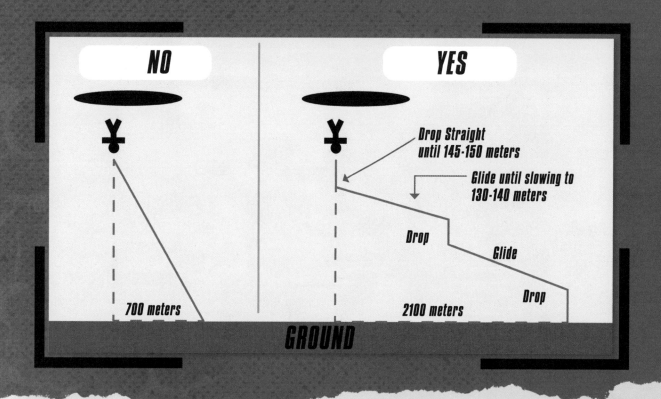

NO

YES

Drop Straight until 145-150 meters

Glide until slowing to 130-140 meters

Drop

Glide

Drop

700 meters

2100 meters

GROUND

> Pay Attention to What Other Teams are Doing

Even if you're not the Jumpmaster, you can still make yourself useful to your team. Activate the free-look function as you drop (by holding L2/LT on PS4 and Xbox One, or right-clicking on PC). You'll be able to monitor other teams and give a heads-up to the Jumpmaster about their locations.

You don't want to head for the same area as multiple other teams. Oh no! Too risky at the beginning. You want to be alert to opportunities to ambush opponents who aren't paying attention to their surroundings. Caution and attention are the keys. Either way, feed as much information to your Jumpmaster as you can.

> Split Up but Don't Wander Too Far!

Stick with your team through the majority of the jump, then break away (press square on PS4, X on Xbox One, Ctrl on PC) when you're roughly 200 meters from the ground. While you want to stay close enough to your squad mates to lend a hand in an emergency, you'll lose out on valuable loot if you stick together at the hip once on the ground. In the first few minutes of the game, load up on equipment by yourself, but be ready to rejoin the group if trouble arises.

Maximizing Jump Distance

As discussed, the least popular locations tend to be the locations that are most distant from the drop ship's randomized path at the start of each game. Players may not have the free-fall skills to reach a far-flung, isolated area.

In other cases, they may not have the patience to wait for the drop ship to carry them closer to a popular destination. Particularly when a well-executed jump can get them there faster.

These are the reasons you need to get good at jumping. If you're just pointing your character to where you want to go and hoping for the best, you're doing it wrong. That's why the wave drop is a very improtant technique to know.

Don't Stray Too Close to Structures or Ground

Stay clear of rock formations and buildings while dropping. If you don't, you may accidentally trigger the landing animation, taking yourself out of the air sooner than you intended.

That said, if your landing target is directly below, you might want to steer close to a rock formation. This will deactivate your boot jets and trigger a free fall—a much quicker way to reach the ground.

> Launch Sooner, Not Later

You may be tempted to stay in the drop ship until it carries you all the way to your target, but if you use the strategies described earlier to maximize your jump distance, it's almost always faster to get there using wave drop than to drop straight down after waiting for the slow drop ship to make its way to the location you want.

> The Old Land n' Slide

You can—and should—slide the instant you hit the ground. You'll get a burst of speed that makes you a tough target for opponents. In the movement section of this guide, we discuss the critical importance of mastering the slide motion.

MOVEMENT

It can't be stressed enough: Apex Legends is a FAST game. The incredible agility of each player avatar makes downing an opponent harder than ever—unless you've mastered movement techniques that he doesn't.

> *Sprinting is for Noobs. Try Sliding!*

What sprinting is to Fortnite, slide-jumping is to Apex Legends.

When covering distances, get in the habit of sprinting into a slide, jumping at the end, then repeating. Sliding is substantially faster than running, and by timing a jump at the very end of a slide you can start a new one. You'll travel through the air at your sliding speed and squeeze out a little more distance. This may not sound like much, but in a battle royale, every inch counts. The terrain of Apex Legends features lots of hills and starting a slide on a downward slope is a great way to traverse long distances quickly.

Don't forget that you can do battle even when you're sliding: You can aim and fire, or even hit melee (more on this later) and pull off a sweet uppercut attack.

> You Move Faster with Weapons Holstered

As in many other first-person shooters, you move slightly faster in Apex Legends with your gun holstered. Of course, there is a risk in putting away your weapon, as the time required to draw it again may be the difference between life and death. So, while we don't recommend exploring high-activity areas with your weapon holstered, you might want to consider doing so when covering a wide-open space that gives you plenty of advance warning of an oncoming enemy.

> No Lying Down on the Job

Apex Legends has done away with the option to lie on your stomach, though you can still crouch. This is in keeping with the general philosophy of the game, which encourages active movement rather than finding a quiet spot to snipe other players. For all intents and purposes, there are no quiet spots in Apex Legends, so no lying down and let's go!

> Characters Move at the Same Speed (Really)

When Apex Legends first launched, many players were convinced that the different Legends moved at different speeds. Given that the different Legends have different sizes, abilities, and hitboxes, this was a fair assumption: The bulkier Legends, like Gibraltar, do appear to move more slowly. Turns out this is just an illusion created by movement animation and the varying heights of player POV from the ground. The developers have officially clarified that the game's characters all walk, run, sprint, and slide at exactly the same speed. So while there are definitely advantages to picking one Legend over another, default speed is not one of them.

Note: We say "default speed" here because certain Legends, including Bangalore and Octane, do possess special speed-boost abilities.

⟩ *Zip Lines Work in Both Directions*

Zip lines are a handy way to cover a lot of ground quickly. You can even attack while zipping along, if your reflexes are fast enough. Unfortunately, you can't change of weapon and manage inventory while on a zip line.

In defiance of the law of gravity, zip lines in Apex Legends allow players to travel in both directions. Players can even switch in mid-zip simply by facing in the opposite direction.

Note that one of the Legends, Pathfinder, can create zip lines for himself and his teammates, a valuable asset in a game that, like Fortnite, places a premium on securing the high ground.

⟩ *Cut Your Zip Trip Short*

You can jump off a zip line at any point on your journey. No need to ride it to the bitter end. It all depends on your destination goal or if you just want to ride the zipline for fun.

> Hot-Air Balloons

Some zip lines soar high into the sky, to a red hot-air balloon which is situated high enough to activate your rocket boots and set you gliding just like you did at the start of the game. Take advantage of the opportunity to cover a good chunk of distance: Before you reach the ground, execute a wave drop or two. Holster your gun first, and you'll go even farther.

Hot-air balloons are extremely useful for moving to new zones, re-entering the shrinking circle of game play, or simply escaping danger. Bear in mind that they can also carry you far away from the protection of your teammates.

One note: If you're riding a zip line to a hot-air balloon, you must ride completely to the top before disengaging from the zip line, or your rocket boots won't redeploy.

> No Fall Damage!

A much-celebrated feature of Apex Legends is the fact that players NEVER suffer damage from a fall, no matter its height. This feature is in keeping with the game's focus on superhuman agility and stunts; it also eliminates a major element of battle-royale strategy. You can fall from the highest cliff and hit the ground running—and so can the enemy. Keep that in mind.

> Don't Let Doors Slow You Down

You can melee-attack doors open or blow them up with a grenade. You can also destroy doors with multiple melee attacks if you want them out of the way.

Why would you want to destroy a poor, helpless door? Doors can be a pain, as downed enemy players can crawl in front of them, block them, and trap you on the other side. But keeping a door intact might be a good strategy if you're hunkered down defending a building. The sound they make when they open can alert you to an enemy's arrival.

> You Can Climb Higher Than You Think

Though Apex Legends exists in the Titanfall universe, the game doesn't feature unfortunately wall-running. But you can climb surprisingly high—up to four times your player avatar's height.

Here's how: Spring toward a wall and hold the jump button while aiming up. With practice, you'll be able to climb to areas that may have seemed out of reach. And in a game where the high ground is everything, that's a skill largely worth practicing!

 Note that you can climb slightly higher with your gun holstered. Use your judgment as to whether it's a safe enough environment to do so.

> *Just Hangin'*

When climbing up a wall, you don't have to immediately vault over the top edge. You can hang from the edge and peek over the top to see what's happening before you commit. Which you really should do, because an opponent could be lying in wait for you on the other side. Look before you leap—literally!

> Auto-run

Apex Legends doesn't have an official auto-run setting, but if you start a sprint and open the menu, your player will continue running in the direction he's pointed in. You can organize inventory and maintain a moving target at the same time (though you can't steer). The key is to choose a direction that won't send you into danger!

> Move Constantly

A moving target is much harder to hit. Get into the habit of constantly moving your character, slowing down only to loot. Make sure you're never caught standing still. Everybody is a target in Apex Legends. But you don't want to be someone's practice target.

> Move Erratically

When running or sliding in the open, use a zigzag pattern to make yourself less vulnerable to long-distance fire. Anything you can do to make it more difficult for opponents to predict where you'll be next is worth your time and effort. Discover which evasive maneuvers come to you most intuitively and practice them. Eventually, they'll be second nature.

> Wiggle It

While looting, your character has to stay relatively still. This is unavoidable, even if it exposes you to danger. But you can make the best of it by "wiggling" your joystick back and forth: This will make your player move slightly. Get into the habit of doing this. Note that the game doesn't allow you to wiggle while respawning a teammate.

> Be Aware of Your Environment

Yes, sound will give you clues about where your enemies are, but there is no substitute for visual information. As you travel, get into the habit of surveying your surroundings, looking for movement in the distance. Don't rely on your map, keep an eye out because your opponents will show no mercy.

> Heal on the Go

While it's not advised to try healing in the thick of a firefight, you can move while you heal. Once you've reached temporary safety, get that heal going, but keep covering ground. DO. NOT. STAND. STILL! Think of yourself as a shark who has to keep moving or die. Be a shark and save yourself!

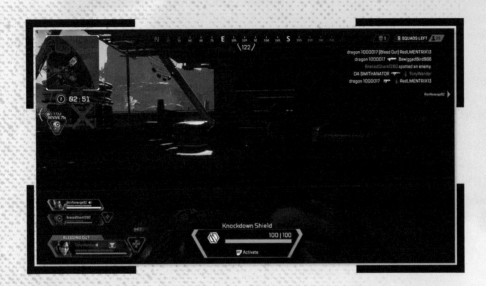

COMBAT

Combat is everything in Apex Legends. For the reasons we've cited—its small map, team-based structure, and increased player mobility—you'll find yourself fighting in Apex a LOT. Here are some tips to improve your combat skills.

➤ *Maximum Health is 200 . . . Keep It That Way*

A dead player with a pocket ful of loot is still dead. Worse, your opponents will now have access to your precious unused items. Get in the mindset of keeping your player not just at 100 health, but at 100 shield too, for a total of 200.

➤ *Know Your Melee*

Let's be honest, if you're down to fisticuffs in a battle royale, things haven't been going your way. But with 30 damage points per hit, melee attacks are better than nothing.

Melee is useful early in matches, when you land too close to a rival group and nobody has weapons yet. Melee attacks are useful for destroying doors too. And they're a great way to conserve ammo when finishing off a downed opponent or destroying Apex bots for loot.

Activate melee by pressing V on the keyboard for PC, and by clicking the right thumb stick on PS4 and Xbox One. There are actually a few different melee attacks in Apex Legends, and all of them do some damage.

❯ Standard Melee

Nothing out of the ordinary here—just a plain old punch in the face. Rock 'em, sock 'em. Tried and true. Your body is a weapon! Use it!

❯ Kick

Your melee attack switches to a kick whenever you're in the air, so you can pull this one off in the midst of jumping or falling. While this attack does the exact same damage as the standard melee, its animation is faster, which means you can get in slightly more damage. The difference is pretty small, but why not get into the habit of kicking? After all, this is Apex Legends. Every second counts.

❯ Uppercut

You'll launch an uppercut when you trigger a melee attack in the middle of a slide. It looks cool, but why not jump at the end of your slide, and trigger the slightly faster kick melee instead?

❯ Finisher

You can trigger a "finisher" by pressing the "interact" button when you're beside a downed enemy. This will execute your opponent in spectacular way but it will also make your character vulnerable to attack for a short time.

It can be worth the risk. Aside from looking rad (there are many flashy variations you can unlock from the Apex store), finishers save precious ammo. And if you've equipped a gold (legendary-tier) shield, a finisher will recharge it to 100%. So if the coast is clear, go for it!

Claim the High Ground

As in any battle royale, the high ground is key in Apex Legends. An elevated position gives you better angles for head shots and more cover from attack; it can also confer a psychological advantage. Learn how to maximize your climbing distance. Use zip lines effectively. Take advantage of hot-air balloons. Claim the high ground and rain death down on your opponents.

> *Be Aggressive, but Pick Your Battles*

In a game like Apex Legends, the old axiom that the best defense is a good offense is painfully true. Apex Legends rewards aggressive play. Execute your attacks with swift and unrelenting speed. Devise your strategy in advance to leave the enemy scrambling to defend itself.

But try to maintain a global awareness of what's happening in the game too. That team you're keen to attack might be facing opposition from other opponents. You may want to hang back until both teams are engaged, emerging only when it's time to mop up the survivors.

If it makes tactical sense to hang back for a second, do it. Never engage in a fight you can't win. Don't be afraid to retreat. And get in the habit of healing so you can fight another day.

> Headshots

Headshots are the Holy Grail of first-person-shooters, offering the highest damage. In Apex Legends, headshots multiply typical body-shot damage by a factor of 1.5 to 2, depending on your weapon. Conversely, shooting a player in the leg does less damage than a body shot.

That said, landing a shot is better than missing entirely, so in certain cases, you may prioritize a shot that inflicts less damage. Your opponent may have found a helmet. Or you may be battling Legends like Bangalore and Octane, whose speed-enhancing abilities make them particularly difficult to hit.

> Give Your Teammates Breathing Room

It's important to work in concert with your teammates and to stick close to one another. But you don't want to stick too close. If you do, you may make the whole team vulnerable—to the splash damage of a grenade or a legendary character's tactical ability.

> Sound Cues Work Best with Headphones

Sound cues are a critical tactical component of this game. Some players even turn off voice communication with their squad, relying directly on ping communication so they can focus on environmental sound cues. Here are some useful cues to listen for:

- Shields breaking: shattering sound
- Voices from the Void (if your player avatar is Wraith):
  whispered warning that enemies are targeting you or close traps
- Apex robots: clinking of their metal feet on the ground
- Ping communications from teammates: various voice prompts
- Incoming supply drop: voice prompt
- Enemy nearby: footsteps
- Doors: hinges creaking open

> Practice Playing to Fight, Not to Win

If your combat skills are lacking, why not try some matches where you immediately head for the supply ship or the hot zone and see how long you last? Don't be afraid; throw caution to the wind and, for the sake of refining your skills, pick fights with all comers.

Sure, by neglecting looting and teamwork, you'll probably be eliminated super-fast, but you can get in a lot of practice. At the end, you must think long-term survival and it's more useful.

> *Take Advantage of Alternate Fire Modes*

A small handful of weapons in Apex Legends have a secondary fire mode. These weapons are:

- R-301 Carbine: full-auto/semi-auto
- VK-47 Flatline: full-auto/semi-auto
- Hemlock Rifle: 3-round burst/semi-auto
- Prowler Burst PDW: 3-round burst/full auto (with the Selectfire hop-up attachment)

Switching from full-auto to semi-auto (burst fire) increases the versatility of these weapons. For example, when firing from a distance, switching to burst mode will conserve ammo. But in close quarters—for example, inside buildings—full auto will enable you to put down an opponent faster, even if it burns more bullets.

> *Think Twice Before Chasing*

If another team retreats, don't chase them automatically. Many teams will have fallback protocol, which can include laying down traps or regrouping at a second hunker-down point. Blind pursuit opens you up to a deadly counterattack.

But chasing can make sense at certain times (it depends), such as when your team has separated a single player from their squad. Chasing and attacking from several angles will make short work of a stray player.

And if you have the time to send out fast-moving players as decoys, you can lead a fleeing opponent directly into the sights of your waiting teammates.

To sum up, assess the situation first, always with a view to what will give you the best odds of long-term survival.

> Don't Always Aim Straight Ahead

Since the aiming reticle is linked to your direction of sight, you may be tempted to "aim" toward where you are going. But try to get into the habit of keeping danger in your sights instead, and strafe your way toward your intended destination. For example, you can move laterally while keeping an eye on the enemies. Make yourself a harder target to hit, and stay aware of your surroundings.

> Shoot From the Hip

Hipfire (shooting without aiming first) is substantially more accurate in Apex Legends than in most other first-person shooter games. With a short-range weapon like a shotgun, save time and use hipfire for enemies less than 10 meters away. First to shoot, first to kill.

> Stay Covered

When you have an enemy on the ropes, you may be tempted to "push," or get closer to him for the *coup de grace*—but remember that fortunes can change very quickly in Apex Legends.

Before rushing your opponent, consider the angles of attack you may be exposing yourself to. Leaving a position with only one line of sight leaves you vulnerable. Remember, the player you're targeting has two teammates out there somewhere, and that they may be waiting for you to make a mistake like this.

> Tactical Reloads

Get into the habit of tactical reloads—reloading when you still have some shots left. You want to have a full clip as much of the time as possible, so if there's a break in combat, use it to reload as you reposition. For most guns, this will be faster than reloading from an empty magazine (which is another reason not to run your ammo dry).

At the same time, don't get so addicted to tactically reloading that you find yourself doing it mid-battle. And bear in mind that you can't reload a gold-tier weapon: Once you've emptied, you should simply throw it away.

 One note: Switching weapons is actually faster than reloading. In certain situations, like frantic skirmishes, it may benefit you to fire your weapon until you've emptied it, then simply switch to another one.

> Don't Forget Your Legendary Abilities

Try to think of each of your legendary abilities as a kind of weapon. Make sure they're adequately charged. But they do recharge continually throughout the game, so don't feel like you have to save them for a rainy day.

> Damage

Damage numbers when you attack an opponent give valuable information in Apex Legends, not only telling you how effective your attack was on a numerical basis, but also changing color depending on their status. These colors are:

GOLDEN YELLOW Successful headshot	PURPLE The player is wearing level 3 armor	BLUE The player is wearing level 2 armor	WHITE The player is wearing level 1 armor	RED The player has no shields remaining

Generally speaking, if the opponent is showing red damage numbers and you have a shield of any kind, you should push in and finish the job, if possible.

> Be Strategic About Downed Enemies

Your may be tempted to finish off a player you've worked hard to put down, but consider holding off. The downed player can't harm you at this point, and their teammates may suspend an attack to try to revive them. You can use the downed player as bait, then hit his teammates, who are vulnerable during the reviving process.

> Don't Forget About Grenades

Many players don't like grenades; the throwing accuracy of this weapon can be difficult to master. But grenades have a variety of important uses, even if they don't take off a single hit point. Frag and thermite grenades throw up dust and flame which can obscure an enemy's view. Tossing a grenade into a choke point may force the enemy back, giving you breathing room. And a well-timed random explosion can usefully distract the enemy.

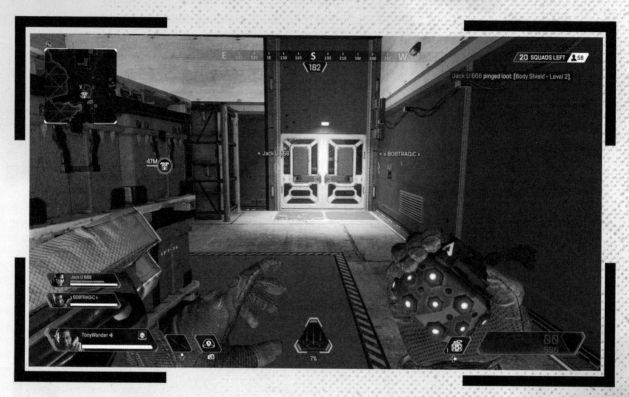

> Bullets Take Time to Travel (with one exception)

Most weapons in Apex Legends (somewhat) obey the physical laws governing velocity over distances. If you shoot a pistol at a player 100 meters away, you can expect a delay before the bullet reaches the target. What, then, are the implications for aiming?

If a player is running or sliding, try to aim at where they WILL be at the time the bullet arrives. This isn't an exact science, and it's slightly different from weapon to weapon. Practice with your favorite firearms to develop an instinct for how far to lead with your aim.

Please note that there's currently only one weapon that is an exception to this rule: The Havoc rifle reaches its target instantaneously.

> Bullets Also Obey Gravity

Players who favor sniper rifles are probably familiar with the concept of "bullet drop": Basically, the more distant the target, the more gravity works on the bullet. So you should aim higher at targets that are farther away. As different weapons in the game have different degrees of bullet drop, take the time to experiment with the weapon of your choice to get a feel for this.

> Aim Drift

Aim drift means that most weapons will start to wobble if you hold down the aim button for too long. Learn to shoot quickly; the window before aim drift begins is brief. You can find stock attachments to minimize aim drift, as discussed in the *Attachments* section.

> Your Sniper Rifle is Also a Set of Binoculars

While the gameplay mechanics of Apex Legends don't exactly encourage sniping, the sniper rifle can be useful simply for its scope. When you're about to traverse an open area, take a moment to scan the far side for movement and activity with your superior zoom power.

> Don't Let Missed Shots Get in Your Head

Maybe you're having an off day and have missed some easy shots. Rather than getting frustrated or tense, take a few deep breaths and let it go. Psychological fortitude plays a big part in a battle royale.

> Take a Break

Get up every half hour and move your real body. You'd be surprised how much a little physical exercise will help you in-game. Take some deep breaths, do some jumping jacks, fill your lungs with oxygen. The game will still be there when you get back.

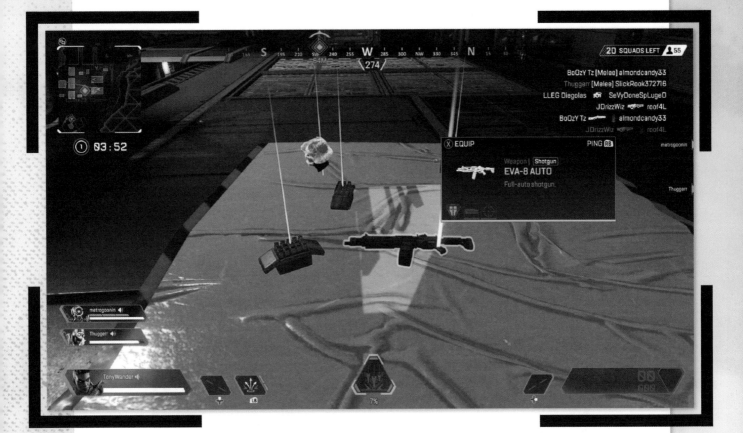

LOOTING

Looting is a major component of this game. You won't get very far in Apex Legends without weapons or gear. During the mad rush of the early game, when players are seeking out the best stuff for their teams, effective looting will give you a crucial competitive edge.

> Looting Sources

Loot isn't exactly hard to find, but the high-tier stuff can be. Here are some tips on how, and where, to loot like a champion.

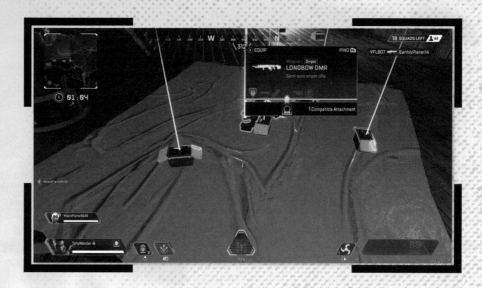

> Supply Bins

Supply-bin locations are fixed and unchanging, as are the number of pieces of loot they contain: three, always randomized. Memorize the locations of these supply bins to loot as efficiently as possible.

> Floor Loot

Floor loot appears randomly, so keep an eye out for it while you're busy seeking out supply bins. This loot is often lower-tier, but in the early game, everything is worth picking up. Better to arm yourself than to leave a weapon lying around for an enemy to pick up. You can always drop the weapon for something better later in the game.

> Apex Robots (Ticks)

Destroy these cute roaming robots to seize the loot they contain. They appear randomly, so listen for the distinct clinking noise they make and smash them with a melee attack.

> Lifeline's Care Packages

As we said previously, Lifeline's ultimate ability enables her to call down extra gear for her squad. Lifeline's loot is mostly defensive, but can include high-tier attachments and even weapons. Reminder: The care-package drop will go quickly and directly to Lifeline's team, so rival players won't really have a chance at it.

> Supply Drops

Once the match gets going, supply drops will occur, accompanied by an audio cue, at map locations identified with a small circle. Supply drops offer randomly selected high-tier loot in small quantities.

Supply drops are also great targets of opportunity, so if a supply drop happens to spawn near you, it's worth your time to head over before other squads arrive. But always assess a supply-drop location before running in. You don't want to be on the wrong side of an ambush.

> Supply Ship

When it reaches its destination, the supply ship deploys zip lines to allow access to it from the ground, but many players try to land on it sooner, just after they leave the drop ship. Like the hot zone, the supply ship is a sought-after looting location, so be prepared to fight for the high-tier stuff.

> The Hot Zone

As discussed in *The Drop* section, the Hot Zone is simply a highlighted area in the map where the chances of finding rarer loot are the best. Every single player in the game is aware of its location, so expect not only impressive loot in the hot zone, but also seriously stiff competition.

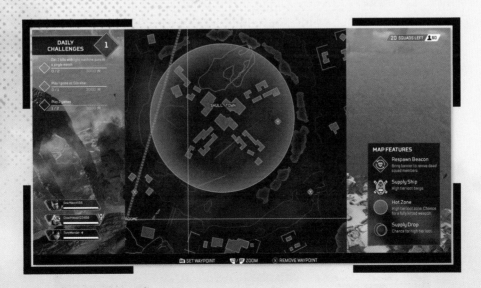

> Death Boxes

An eliminated player will leave behind a "death box" you can pilfer. The box will be color-coded according to the highest-tier loot inside, allowing you to assess whether it's worth stopping to claim it.

Those colors, and their respective meanings, are discussed later in this section.

> Flyers

These creatures are a new addition to Apex Legends Season 2. They carry death boxes that can be shot down to collect valuable loot. They are large, i.e. the size of a pterodactyl, and have a parasitic relationship with Leviathans, latching onto them and generally hanging around the larger creature. They are powerful enough to rip through ship armour, though at this stage in the game they do not attack players. They fly in a circle which makes it easier to predict their flight path, and they can be shot so that they drop their death boxes without killing them. Killing them requires doing 250 HP damage.

> *Loot Rarity*

Loot occurs in Apex Legends in four tiers of rarity. In general, the rarity corresponds to the quality of the looted item. For example, a body shield of white rarity will recharge only 50 hit points, whereas the purple-rarity version will restore full shields. Knowing which colors are most valuable will help you prioritize certain loot over others, enabling you to think on your feet and saving you precious time.

> *White (Common)*

The most basic tier offers underwhelming loot, but in the early game, beggars can't be choosers.
As you progress through the game and accumulate a cache of better weapons and gear, you can start passing over loot in this rarity tier.

> *Blue (Rare)*

Blue-tier loot is middle of the road, and often worth picking up until late game. Do not neglect it.

> *Purple (Epic)*

This tier offers the highest statistics, and is almost always worth checking out— unless you're pleased with your loadout and believe it could only be improved with gold-tier weapons.

> Gold (Legendary)

Gold-tier loot offers the same stats as its purple-tier equivalents, but with special enhancements. For example, gold body armor offers the ability to fully recharge your shield after performing a finisher on an enemy. This type of loot is HIGHLY sought after, extremely advantageous, and very much worth fighting for.

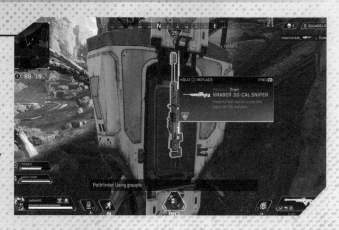

GENERAL LOOTING TIPS

> Loot Smart

Thoroughly review the *Weapons, Attachments, Items, and Gear* sections of this guide to instantly identify whether a piece of loot is of value to you. Remember that you're at your most vulnerable when looting, so make sure you only take risks that are worthwhile.

> Stay Frosty

No piece of loot is worth getting killed over. Remember that other teams may lie in wait. If you have Legends that are skilled in reconnaissance on your team, use them to check out the territory and gather information.

> Use Loot as Bait

If you're sitting pretty with equipment, you may choose to use loot locations tactically, camping out near a supply drop to ambush other squads.

> Ping Loot You Don't Want

We'll discuss pinging in greater detail in the *Team Work* section, but remember to ping any items you're leaving behind. If every player on a team gets into the habit of sharing information in this way, you'll maximize looting efficiency.

> Watch for the Red Slash

A red slash next to an inventory item indicates one of two things: You already have one, or you don't own the weapon it's an attachment for. Leave behind incompatible items unless you have a very good reason to do otherwise (for example, a high-tier sniper-rifle attachment may inspire you to seek out that sniper rifle).

> Don't Always Loot the Same Way

If you have the option of looting a location from the roof down, do it. Most players will start at the bottom of a building and work their way up. Imagine their surprise when they run smack into you, fully equipped and ready to punish them for their obliviousness.

WEAPONS

Like all battle royales, Apex Legends is fundamentally a game about weapons: coveting them, finding them, firing them. As of Season 1 and Season 2, the game offers a bit more than twenty weapons, though if you take attachments into account, the number of variations is massive. This section will examine all of this equipment in detail and offer you some guidance in choosing a loadout for your character.

GENERAL WEAPON TIPS

> The First Magazine Is Free...

Every new weapon you pick up includes one magazine, so even if you don't find any more ammo with it, at least you'll get to use it a few times before you have to think about replenishing it.

> Attachments Are Key

Weapons quickly become more powerful as you add attachments to them. Familiarize yourself with the various attachments that are available in Apex Legends, and trick out your gun; make it top-notch. A couple of solid attachments can take a gun from so-so to so awesome.

It's crucial, once you've chosen and committed to your weapon, to make your teammates aware—verbally and/or via ping—that you're hunting for the attachments that will upgrade it.

> Auto Attach

Attachments automatically attach themselves to the weapon they're designed for, saving you time. If you have several applicable weapons, the new attachment you've found will prioritize the one that has a free slot. If you have multiple weapons with free slots, the attachment will prioritize the one you've equipped. You can customize attachments in the inventory screen.

> Sniping 101

The design and function of sniper rifles in Apex Legends are mathematically precise, to a degree that can be surprising. This means that if you make your calculations properly, you can place a bullet hundreds of meters away with pretty remarkable accuracy. Here's how:

- Each hash mark on your ranged scope represents 100 meters of distance.
- When you aim through a scope, the game will tell you what the exact distance is between you and your target.
- It's a simple calculation to aim higher than the target: Go up one hash mark for every 100 meters.
- For example, if the target is 250 meters away, you'll line it up not with the crosshairs, but halfway between the second and third hash mark above the crosshairs. Boom—accurate shots, every time.

> Top weapons

Most of the Apex Legends weapons are pretty powerful once they're outfitted with good attachments, but the general consensus is that these, below, are the best in each category. Loot well, loot often, and keep an eye out for them!

- Peacekeeper (shotgun)
- R-301 Carbine (assault rifle)
- R-99 (submachine gun)

- M600 Spitfire (light machine gun)
- Wingman (pistol)
- Arc Star grenade (sticky grenade)

And just for fun, be aware that the worst weapon in the game is the infamous Mozambique shotgun.

SPECIFIC WEAPONS

Assault Rifles

These are must-haves in Apex Legends, as they're great medium-range weapons that dish out decent damage at a fast rate, even as they're fairly forgiving in the aiming department. Currently, Apex Legends has four assault rifles (we're including the Havoc for simplicity, even though it's an energy-based weapon).

Name	Havoc	VK-47 Flatline	Hemlock Burst AR	R-301 Carabine
Ammo	Energy Ammo	Heavy Rounds	Heavy Rounds	Light Rounds
Magazine Size	25	20	18	18
Tactical Reload/ Full Reload	3,20 s/3,20 s	2,40 s/3,10 s	2,40 s/2,80 s	2,40 s/3,20 s
DPS (Damages Per Second)	201,6	160	108	189
Body/Head/Leg Damages	18/36/13,5	19/32/12	18/36/13.5(Per Burst: 54/108/40.5)	14/28/10,5
Fire Rate SPS (Shots Per Second)	11.2 (1.7 in single-shot mode)	10	15 (6 including downtime between bursts)	13,5
Attachment Slots	Optic, Stock, Hop-up	Mag, Optic, Stock	Barrel, Mag, Optic, Stock	Barrel, Mag, Optic, Stock
Modes	Auto, Single (with Hop-up)	Single, Auto	Single, Burst (3-shot)	Single, Auto
Projectile Speed	30 500	26 000	27 500	29 000
Draw Time	0,60 s	0,60 s	0,60 s	0,60 s

Aiming Down Sight Movement Speed (% of non-ADS speed)	50 %	50 %	50 %	50 %

> Havoc

The Havoc is a great example of a weapon that lives or dies according to the attachments it's tricked out with. Without any attachments, this gun takes time to "wind up," which makes it both awkward to use and a real ammo-eater. But the turbocharger attachment eliminates this drawback:

Suddenly, the Havoc becomes a formidable weapon. You can also use the Selectfire Receiver attachment to transform the Havoc into a laser weapon. On the one hand, a laser weapon has the advantage of not suffering from bullet travel. It instantaneously hits the target and does not drop from gravity as well. On the other, it takes time to charge, which basically nullifies the advantage of no bullet travel.

> VK-47 Flatline

This is a perfectly fine weapon, definitely the middle of the road in terms of Apex Legends assault rifles. Its large clip size and decent damage makes it a good choice as an early-game weapon, especially for a new player. And it only gets better with attachments.

> Hemlock

This is a burst weapon, which means it fires bursts of three bullets. In the hands of a capable marksman, it can be deadly, dealing 100 damage points in a quarter of a second. Its damage per shot is quite high, equal to the Havoc's, but without that annoying wind-up time. That said, the players have spoken, and the most popular assault rifle in the game is...

> R-301 Carbine

Widely considered to be one of the best assault rifle Apex Legends has produced so far, the R-301 carbine has low recoil, high bullet velocity, and a fast rate of fire. Gussied up with some decent attachments, this can be a very versatile weapon for short range and—if you switch over to single-shot mode—even long range.

Submachine Guns (SMGs)

Submachine guns occupy an awkward niche in the weapons category, as they are less effective for long-range fighting than assault rifles, and don't pack as much of a punch, at close range, as shotguns. Still, in the early game you have to take what the loot gods bestow upon you, and an SMG will serve as a great placeholder until you find yourself a good assault rifle.

Name	Alternator	R99	Prowler Burst PDW
Ammo	Light Rounds	Light Rounds	Heavy Rounds
Magazine Size	16	18	20
Tactical Reload/Full Reload	1.90s/2.23s	1.80s/2.45s	2.00s/2.60s
DPS (Damages Per Second)	130	216	122.78
Body/Head/Leg Damages	15/19/10.4	12/18/9.6	14/21/11.2
Fire Rate SPS (Shots Per Second)	10	18	20 (8.77 including downtime between bursts)
Attachment Slots	Barrel, Mag, Optic, Stock, Hop-up	Barrel, Mag, Optic, Stock	Mag, Optic, Stock, Hop-up
Modes	Auto	Auto	Burst (5-shot)
Projectile Speed	19500	21000	18000
Draw Time	0.35s	0.35s	0.35s
ADS Movement Speed (% of non-ADS speed)	86%	86%	86%

> Alternator

The Alternator fires fairly slowly, but has a great reload time and not much recoil. You could certainly do worse than this weapon for an early-game companion.

> R-99

The R-99 is a better investment than the Alternator because of its fast fire rate. But a limited clip size and high recoil rate means that you'll definitely need attachments to make this weapon viable in battle. Without attachments, what you've got is a gun that absolutely burns through ammo and can't easily

be aimed. But if you're willing to put the effort into outfitting it the way it needs to be outfitted, you'll end up with one of the very best weapons Apex Legends has to offer.

> Prowler Burst PDW

This is another SMG that won't turn many heads without certain essential attachments. Equipped with the hop-up attachment, for instance, this weapon can really dole out some damage with its five-shot burst mode. Like the Alternator, the Prowler is an investment, which is to say a risk, because most

people would favor an R-99 to take up that precious weapon slot. But if you're committed to finding and equipping the right attachments, this is definitely a great weapon.

Light Machine Guns (LMGs)

It's strange that the word "light" is part of the name of the LMG, because this weapon is both heavier and more powerful than an assault rifle. Its benefits are an increased rate of fire and higher damage; the drawbacks that offset those benefits include a substantial wind-up period, which can be extremely annoying. Still, this is a great class of weapon.

Name	Devotion	M600 Spitfire	L-Star EMG
Ammo	Energy Ammo	Heavy Rounds	Unique Ammo
Magazine Size	44	35	40 (x3)
Tactical Reload/Full Reload	2.80s/3.63s	2.80s/3.33s	3.26s/3.26s
DPS (Damages Per Second)	255	180	252
Body/Head/Leg Damages	17/34/12.75	20/40/16	21/42/17
Fire Rate SPS (Shots Per Second)	15 (at max)	9	12
Attachment Slots	Barrel, Optic, Stock, Hop-up	Barrel, Mag, Optic, Stock	None
Modes	Auto (Wind-Up)	Auto	Auto (overheat)
Projectile Speed	33500	27500	18000
Draw Time	0.70s	0.70s	0.70s
ADS Movement Speed (% of non-ADS speed)	41%	41%	41%

> Devotion

This weapon has a great rate of fire and high damage per second. But its Achilles' heel is a brutal wind-up time that makes operating the gun a massive headache. That said, a turbocharger hop-up attachment will shorten the warm-up period. Without this attachment, the gun is basically useless in attacks at close range: By the time it finally gets rolling, you're probably dead from multiple shotgun blasts to the skull.

Note: This weapon takes energy ammo, which is a less common form of loot. So if you settle on a Devotion as your weapon of choice, make sure to stay in contact with your teammates so they'll know that you're the guy to whom they should be donating any and all energy ammo they stumble onto.

> L-Star EMG

The L-Star EMG is a rare and pretty spectacular light machine gun that's new to Apex Legends as of Season 2. By general consensus, it has deposed the Devotion as the game's best LMG.

The L-Star has a magazine capacity of 40 rounds and is arguably a more accurate weapon than the Devotion due to its larger projectiles. And it has no wind-up period—a feature that makes it significantly easier to use, not to mention more lethal.

The L-Star has a very high rate of fire, and does substantial damage per shot with its large plasma projectiles. But you can't just mindlessly unload on the enemy: If you aren't careful, the weapon will overheat, rendering it useless for a few seconds (it's the first gun in the game that's susceptible to overheating). Experimentation has shown that you can safely fire in bursts of approximately six to eight shots at a time.

Like the Kraber .50-cal and Mastiff, the L-Star is available only via airdrops and cannot be found in ordinary, ground-based loot locations. This weapon is a no-brainer to add to your loadout, if you're fortunate enough to find one. Just be careful not to overheat in the middle of a firefight and leave yourself vulnerable to a counterattack.

L-Star EMG stats (Time To Kill)

DMG Type	DMG	Shots To Kill	Time To Kill
Bodyshots	21	5/8/9/10	0,33 s/0,58 s/ 0,67 s/0,75 s
Headshots vs No Helmet	42	3/4/5/5	0,17 s/0,25 s/ 0,33 s/0,33 s
Headshots vs Lvl 1 Helmet (10%)	37,8	3/4/5/6	0,17 s/0,25 s/ 0,33 s/0,42 s
Headshots vs Lvl 2 Helmet (20%)	33,6	3/5/6/6	0,17 s/0,33 s/ 0,42 s/0,42 s
Headshots vs Lvl 3/4 Helmet (25%)	31,5	4/5/6/7	0,25 s/0,33 s/ 0,42 s/0,50 s

> M600 Spitfire

This weapon is an absolute beast, boasting 20 damage per shot, and a large magazine size. What does that mean for your bottom line? If you upgrade your magazine attachment and unleash this puppy on an enemy player who boasts full health and shields, you can take them down even if you only land 15% (!) of your shots. In other words, you can miss 85% of the time using the M600 Spitfire and still win in a mano a mano combat engagement. Add what if you add in a barrel stabilizer? Then no one can stop you.

Sniper Rifles

As discussed earlier, Apex Legends is a game that positively discourages sniping. Because of the frantic combat, the smaller map size, and higher mobility of players, playing the long-range game doesn't make a whole lot of sense. But that doesn't mean that a sniper rifle in the right hands can't still be quite useful. At the very least, the scope of a sniper rifle can function as an extremely useful tool for seeing what's what in the medium and long-range distance.

Name	G7 Scout	Longbow DMR	Triple Take	Kraber .50-cal
Ammo	Light Rounds	Heavy Rounds	Energy Ammo	Unique
Magazine Size	10	5	5	4
Tactical Reload/ Full Reload	2.40s/3.00s	2.66s/3.66s	2.60s/3.40s	3.20s/4.30s
DPS (Damages Per Second)	135	66	86.25	150
Body/Head/Leg Damages	30/60/21.75	55/110/39.875	23/46/16.675 (69/138/50.025)	145/250/90.625
Fire Rate SPS (Shots Per Second)	4.5	1.2	1.25	1.2
Attachment Slots	Barrel, Mag, Optic, Stock	Barrel, Mag, Optic, Stock, Hop-up	Optic, Stock, Hop-up	None
Modes	Single	Single	Single (3-shot spread)	Single
Projectile Speed	31500	30500	32000	29500

Draw Time	0.60s	0.90s	0.90s	1.20s
ADS Movement Speed (% of non-ADS speed)	36%	36%	36%	36%

> G7 Scout

The G7 deals less damage than other sniper rifles in Apex Legends, but compensates for it with a high rate of fire. This makes it pretty versatile as a medium-range weapon. But if long-distance combat is your pride and joy, you really can do better than the G7, which requires multiple hits to deal the same damage as individual rounds discharged by the various other sniper rifles in this category.

> Longbow DMR

This sniper rifle packs a punch—nearly double the damage of the G7. A hop-up attachment increases the headshot damage it's capable of inflicting, so if you're good at aiming, it can be decent strictly in its capacity as a dedicated long-distance weapon.

> Triple Take

We have to be frank: This rifle is not very effective for long-distance combat. It has a three-shot spread that—as you would expect—spreads out over a distance. What's weird, though, is that it's unexpectedly good for combat at close range. It's hands-down the best sniper rifle for hipfiring.

But ask yourself this necessary and essential question: Why do you, an Apex Legends superstar-in-training, care about a sniper rifle that's best suited for close-range combat? Answer: You don't.

> Kraber .50-cal

This is one of the two legendary weapons currently available in Apex Legends, and its attributes speak loudly for themselves. It can deal 250 headshot damage in a single shot. It has a built-in high-zoom 10x scope. Does that sound too good to be true? Because it is: You only get the ammo that

comes with this weapon, so the thing is totally and completely useless after eight shots. (Except maybe for keeping a door open on a windy day.) But those eight shots are rare and precious things, each and every one of them is a poem of destruction and mayhem. Don't waste them, cowboy !

Shotguns

Nothing beats a shotgun for close-range, in-your-face combat. Most players won't think twice about reserving one of their precious inventory slots for a good old shotgun. But which one is right for you?

Name	EVA-8 Auto	Peacekeeper	Mozambique	Mastiff
Ammo	Shotgun Shells	Shotgun Shells	Shotgun Shells	Unique
Magazine Size	8	6	3	4
Tactical Reload/Full Reload	2.75s/3.00s	2.50s/3.50s	2.10s/2.60s	1.03s/1.70s
DPS (Damages Per Second)	126	106.7	99	187.2
Body/Head/Leg Damages	7/10/5.6 (63/90/50.4)	10/15/8 (110/165/88)	15/22/13.5 (45/66/40.5)	18/36/18 (144/288/144)
Fire Rate SPS (Shots Per Second)	2	0.97	2.2	1.3
Attachment Slots	Optic, Bolt	Optic, Bolt, Hop-up	Optic, Bolt, Hop-up	None
Modes	Auto	Single	Auto	Single
Projectile Speed	16000	16000	10000	12000
Draw Time	0.45s	0.45s	0.45s	0.45s
ADS Movement Speed (% of non-ADS speed)	91%	91%	100%	91%

> Mozambique

A good weapon gives you the confidence to hunt down enemy players and dispatch them, one by one, to their virtual Maker. A bad weapon makes you want to respawn, just to be put out of your misery. Boy, does this weapon without attachment suck. It's a shotgun/pistol combination that

manages to underperform miserably in both categories. The Apex Legends community considers the Mozambique to be the absolute worst weapon in the game, and it's not even close. So unless it's the very first weapon you find, don't waste any time with it. And dump it at the earliest opportunity that presents itself unless you find a Hammerpoint attachment...

> Mastiff

This is second of the two legendary weapons in Apex Legends as of Season 1. As mentioned earlier, you only get twenty shots with this beast, then it's a doorstop/ paperweight. But you can do a lot with those twenty shots: Each one discharges eight pellets that do 36 damage each. That means that if

you're close enough to your opponent, you can deal out 288 damage with just one pull of the trigger. No wonder the game severely limits how much you can use the Mastiff. It's almost too good.

> Peacekeeper

The players have spoken; let us heed them: This is the best shotgun in the whole game (not including the legendary weapon Mastiff, discussed previously). It has high damage-per-shot, a large and deadly spread pattern, and uses ammo efficiently. If you can find this weapon, hang onto it!

> EVA-8 Auto

This weapon doesn't have a great damage-per-shot rating, but its firing rate is fairly quick, meaning it's a great choice for new players that haven't mastered the hurry-up-and-wait style of shotgun combat. Once you've gotten your chops down—once you're ready to graduate from a beginner-grade weapon— the Peacekeeper is a way better choice.

Pistols

A pistol can be your friend at both close and medium ranges, and it's very much worth its weight during the early stages of an Apex Legends match. As the game progresses, you're likely to switch your allegiance to more specialized weapons—your assault rifles, your shotguns—but the humble pistol still has its uses, and it can get you out of a jam.

Name	P2020	RE-45 Auto	Wingman
Ammo	Light Rounds	Light Rounds	Heavy Rounds
Magazine Size	10	15	6
Tactical Reload/Full Reload	1.25s/1.25s	1.74s/2.12s	2.10s/2.10s
DPS (Damages Per Second)	102	143	117
Body/Head/Leg Damages	13/18/10.8	11/16/9.9	45/90/40.5
Fire Rate SPS (Shots Per Second)	8.5	13	2.6
Attachment Slots	Mag, Optic, Hop-up	Barrel, Mag, Optic, Hop-up	Mag, Optic, Hop-up
Modes	Single	Auto	Single
Projectile Speed	18500	19500	18000
Draw Time	0.25s	0.25s	0.25s
ADS Movement Speed (% of non-ADS speed)	100%	95%	100%

> Wingman

The Wingman is a great pistol if you have the skills to use it the way it's meant to be used. It has a high rate of damage, and an OK rate of fire. What's most impressive about it is that it performs well at close, medium, and long range, making it one of the best all-around guns in the game. Another benefit: It doesn't require attachments out of the gate to perform well, so if you find a Wingman, it will start paying off immediately. Cherish it and keep it close.

> P2020

An all-around disappointment. Don't waste too much time on this weapon unless it's early game and you have zero other options. It has a severely low damage rating; its upside, to the extent it has one, is its relatively high rate of fire. But other weapons will absolutely eat it for breakfast.

> RE-45 Auto

This pistol is fully automatic, but suffers from a significant amount of recoil, both horizontal and vertical. It can be a good pistol for new players, but players with experience will probably avoid it.

Grenades

A lot of players don't bother with grenades, because inflicting damage with this small bomb can be difficult in Apex Legends. But a grenade can be very useful, as we explain in the *Advanced Tips* section of this book. You can stack up to two grenades of any kind in a single inventory slot.

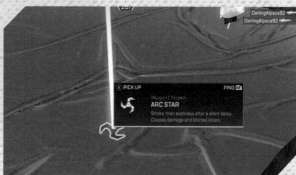

> Arc Star Grenade

The Arc Star is a sticky grenade, which means that it stays put after making contact with an object or player. The moment it hits something, it arms itself; what follows is a three-second countdown, and then baby goes boom! An Arc Star can cause up to 70 damage and will stun players for five seconds. It also disables enemy shields, so fast-moving, quick-thinking players can really make the most of this weapon to move in for a rapid kill.

> Frag Grenade

Like a standard grenade, a frag grenade will roll for a while after hitting the ground. There will be a four-second delay before it explodes. A frag grenade can be used to do damage to enemies as well as to blow the doors of buildings off their hinges.

> Thermite Grenade

A thermite grenade explodes upon impact with a surface (though not when it hits an enemy player). It creates a horizontal line of flames that causes increasing damage to a player who remains in contact with it. This grenade is not optimized for racking up damage to enemy fighters, but it can be deployed to efficiently control areas or to discourage players from pushing in on your position. A thermite grenade will not destroy doors.

ATTACHMENTS

Attachments play a critical part in the management and function of Apex Legends weapons, because they substantially improve the performance of many of the guns featured in the game.

If you pick up an attachment that is compatible with a gun in your inventory, it will automatically attach itself to that gun, saving you the trouble of equipping it.

Attachments, like gear, are available in different tiers, corresponding to the established rarity colors.

An attachment will only equip to a gun with the complementary attachment slot. Watch out for the red slash when you hover over an attachment in your inventory. It's an indication that means none of your current weapons can make use of the attachment.

> Hop-up Attachments

This type of attachment isn't compatible with all weapons: Each hop-up will fit only a specific gun or handful of guns. When a hop-up does fit, however, it offers a significant advantage, and for this reason it's only available in purple and gold rarity tiers.

Name	Attaches To	Variant(s)	Effect(s)
Precision Choke	Peacekeeper, Triple Take	purple	holds ADS for a tighter spread over time
Selectfire Receiver	Prowler, Havoc	purple	enables full-auto firing mode
Skullpiercer Rifling	Longbow, Wingman	gold	increases headshot damage
Turbocharger	Devotion, Havoc	gold	reduces/ removes spin-up time
Disruptor Rounds	Alternator, RE-45	purple	dramatically increases damage to shields only
Hammerpoint	P2020, Mozambique	purple	dramatically increases damage to health only

> Optic Attachments (Sights and Scopes)

Scopes can attach to most guns in the game, and generally allow you to zoom in on enemy targets. Gold scopes are very useful, as they offer threat highlighting, which outlines enemies in red so you can see them, even through smoke or gas. If you have legendary characters such as Caustic or Bangalore on your team, prioritize finding a scope of this type, as it synergizes well with their legendary abilities.

Name	Attaches To	Variant(s)	Effect(s)
1x Holo	all weapons	white	close-range sight
1x Digital Threat	shotguns, SMGs, pistols	gold	close-range sight with threat highlighting
1x-2x Variable Holo	all weapons	blue	close-range variable sight
1x HCOG 'Classic'	all weapons	white	close-range sight
2x HCOG 'Bruiser'	all weapons	blue	close-range sight
3x HCOG 'Ranger'	snipers, LMGs, ARs, SMGs	purple	mid-range sight
2x-4x Variable AOG	snipers, LMGs, ARs, SMGs	purple	mid-range variable sight
6x Sniper	snipers	blue	long-range sight
4x-8x Variable Sniper	snipers	purple	long-range variable sight
4x-10x Digital Sniper Threat	snipers	gold	long-range variable sight with threat highlighting

> Extended Magazines

These attachments simply increase the number of rounds your weapon can hold before you need to reload which can make a huge difference during a skirmish. The higher-rarity versions of these attachments also offer a quicker fire rate and shorter reload time.

Name	Attaches To	Variant(s)	Effect(s)
Extended Light Mag	all light weapons	white, blue, purple, gold	increases ammo capacity (blue and up: reduces reload time)
Extended Heavy Mag	all heavy weapons	white, blue, purple, gold	increases ammo capacity (blue and up: reduces reload time)
Shotgun Bolt	shotguns	white, blue, purple, gold	increases fire rate
Extended Energy Mag	all energy weapons	white, blue, purple, gold	increases ammo capacity (blue and up: reduces reload time)

> Barrel Stabilizer

The barrel stabilizer is a useful attachment that reduces the recoil of your weapon. It works best with high-recoil automatic weapons like assault rifles, light machine guns, and submachine guns. It is available in all rarity colors, each of which incrementally increases its performance. The gold variant also minimizes weapon flash, which can come in handy if you're firing from a concealed position.

Name	Attaches To	Variant(s)	Effect(s)
Barrel Stabilizer	LMGs, RE-45, G7 Scout, Longbow, Alternator, R-99, Hemlock, R-301 Carbine	white, blue, purple, gold	reduces recoil (gold also reduces weapon flash)

> Stock Attachments

A better stock for your weapon has two benefits. It decreases the time you need in order to draw that weapon and, perhaps more importantly, it reduces "aim drift," which is the amount of wobble that occurs when you zoom in to aim. This can be very useful for sniper rifles and other long-distance weapons.

Name	Attaches To	Variant(s)	Effect(s)
Standard Stock	LMGs, SMGs, ARs	white, blue, purple, gold	decreases draw time and reduces aim drift
Sniper Stock	snipers	white, blue, purple, gold	decreases draw time and reduces aim drift

Ammunition

There are four types of ammunition in Apex Legends. Each one is associated with a different color, as follows:

- light rounds – brown
- heavy rounds – green
- shotgun shells – red
- energy ammo – yellow

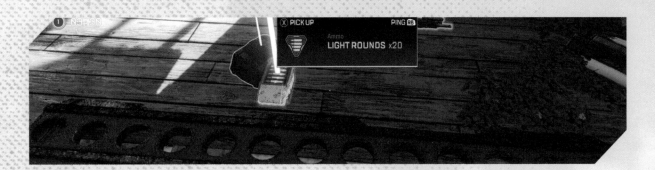

Memorize the different ammunition colors to save time, because there's no point in picking up rounds for weapons you don't carry. While you're at it, make sure to ping any ammo you don't need so your teammates can pick it up if useful.

Remember that gold-tier weapons have their own special ammo, and that they're useless when that ammo runs out. Don't hesitate to dump these weapons to free up some inventory space.

HEALING ITEMS

We need a little respawn over here! There's no time, this is a matter of life or death!

Keeping your hit points up is a major factor in reaching the endgame of an Apex Legends match, and consumables will help you do just that. All of them offer advantages to health or shields except one: the Ultimate Accelerant, which speeds up recharge time for a legendary character's Ultimate Ability. If you have Lifeline on your team, give her the Ultimate Accelerant, as her care packages are by far the most useful Ultimate Ability.

Each different consumable occupies a space in your inventory (though with some you can stack multiples in a single slot). Learn which ones are most valuable so you can choose quickly between a syringe and a medkit during battle.

Note: Shields will suffer damage before health does, until they are shattered—except when you're outside the ring: Being outside the ring depletes health directly, totally bypassing shields.

Stats

Healing Item	Effect	Duration	Drop Stack Size	Max Stack Size
Syringe	restores 25 health	5s	2	6
Medkit	restores 100 health	8s	1	3
Shield Cell	restores 25 health	3s	2	6
Shield Battery	restores 100 health	5s	1	3
Phoenix Kit	restores 100 health and 100 shields	10s	1	1
Ultimate Accelerant	restores 20% Ultimate	7s	1	1

Syringe

Medkit

Shield Cell

Shield Battery

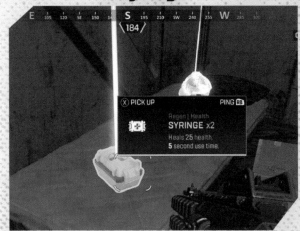

Phoenix Kit

Ultimate Accelerant

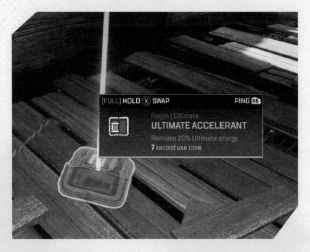

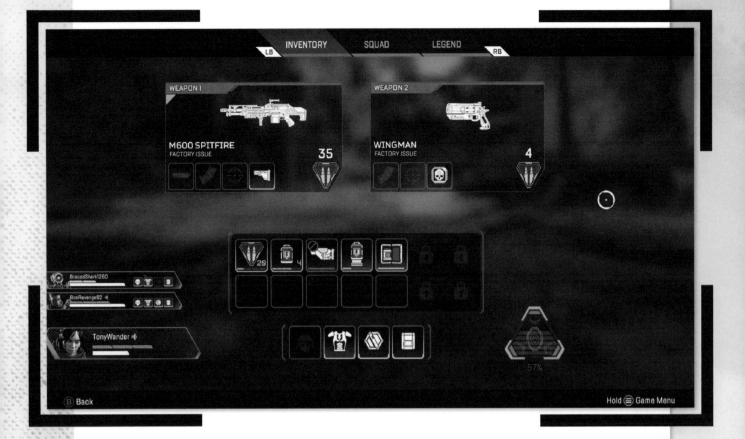

GEAR

Weapons are critically important in Apex Legends, but they aren't everything. To stay alive long enough to use weapons, you need gear. This section will cover all the gear available in the game, along with relevant statistics.

Note that when you review your inventory, a red slash will indicate when a loot isn't compatible with the equipment you're already using. Don't let that stop you from holding onto an attachment for a weapon you hope to come across, but don't hesitate to free up inventory space, either.

> Body Shields

In addition to your base health of 100 points, you can equip body shields, which will maximize your health up to 200 points in increments of 25. Get into the habit of maximizing your shields constantly so you always have 200 hit points to play with. An unused body shield in your inventory can't help you if you're dead!

Gold-tier shields offer the special ability of a full shield recharge every time you perform a finisher on a downed opponent. Considering how difficult it is to stay alive in Apex Legends, this is a pretty awesome perk.

Stats

Name	Rarity	Effect(s)
Body Shield (Level 1)	Common (White)	+50 shield capacity
Body Shield (Level 2)	Rare (Blue)	+75 shield capacity
Body Shield (Level 3)	Epic (Purple)	+100 shield capacity
Body Shield (Level 4)	Legendary (Gold)	+100 shield capacity, and full recharge of shields after successful execution of a finisher on a downed enemy.

> Helmets

A helmet mitigates damage from headshots, according to the rarity of the helmet. The Apex Legends website insists that a helmet limits only "bonus" headshot damage, but field testing has determined that a helmet actually reduces TOTAL headshot damage.

A helmet never breaks or needs to be recharged, so once you've got one, you can breathe a sigh of relief knowing that you're slightly more protected.

A gold-tier helmet increases the speed of tactical and ultimate abilities, so it might be worth handing off this valuable piece of equipment to a squad member with epic ultimate abilities, like Pathfinder.

Stats

Name	Rarity	Effect(s)
Helmets (Level 1)	Common (White)	10% total damage reduction
Helmets (Level 2)	Rare (Blue)	20% total damage reduction
Helmets (Level 3)	Epic (Purple)	25% total damage reduction
Helmets (Level 4)	Legendary (Gold)	25% total damage reduction, and increased charge speed of Tactical and Ultimate abilities.

> Knockdown Shields

This item comes into play when you are "knocked down," i.e., have your health reduced to zero. In this state, you are pretty much helpless, though a teammate can still revive you. That's where knockdown shields come in. When your objective is to survive just long enough to be revived, a knockdown shield creates a barrier between you and enemies who might try to finish you off with gunfire.

Note that knockdown shields don't protect you from an opponent's finisher, so make sure you always crawl in the opposite direction of any enemy who might try to execute one.

The gold-tier knockdown shield is extremely useful, as it allows you one self-revive if you're knocked down. Again, consider donating this item to a teammate whose survival is critical to the health of the whole squad, like Lifeline.

Stats

Name	Rarity	Effect(s)
Knockdown Shield (Level 1)	Common (White)	shield with 100 health
Knockdown Shield (Level 2)	Rare (Blue)	shield with 250 health
Knockdown Shield (Level 3)	Epic (Purple)	shield with 750 health
Knockdown Shield (Level 4)	Legendary (Gold)	shield with 750 health, plus ability to self-revive once if knocked down

> Backpacks

Because they're scarce, inventory slots are extremely valuable in a battle royale. The backpack gives you more of them (for specifics on this, see below). The gold-tier feature of the backpack is that healing items take half as long to use, not bad, isn't it?

Note that if you drop a backpack for a teammate to pick up, the various items contained in the extra slots will also appear on the ground.

Stats

Name	Rarity	Effect(s)
Backpack (Level 1)	Common (White)	+2 inventory slots
Backpack (Level 2)	Rare (Blue)	+4 inventory slots
Backpack (Level 3)	Epic (Purple)	+4 inventory slots
Backpack (Level 4)	Legendary (Gold)	+6 inventory slots, and healing items take half as long to consume

TEAM WORK

A huge part of Apex Legends is working seamlessly with your squad to defeat the other teams. This requires several specialized skills you may not have developed while playing "every man for himself" battle royales. In this section, we'll take a look at how to best synchronize your squad, whether you're best friends or you've just met.

Pick Complementary Legends

Even if you've decided on a favorite Legend, you should try to build up your skills with several different ones. This will allow you to have more flexibility when your team members pick their own characters, since you may not get your first—or, for that matter, even your second—choice. Beyond that, a squad that selects Legends that work together well is going to do better in the game than a squad in which everyone just fights over Wraith. Familiarize yourself with the *Legends* section of this guide and be ready to make a choice that's a good fit with the rest of the group. And if no one's picked Lifeline—well, there's always a need for Lifeline.

Nobody Likes A Lone Wolf

You might be positively awesome at Apex Legends, but no matter how good you are, you won't last long on your own, and your teammates will struggle to succeed without your support. Resist the temptation to go off on your own. Stick with the team. And if you've got all the top loot locations memorized, share the wealth a little. It benefits the whole team if you all have good gear.

Ping Early, and Ping Often

The ping system, enabling teams to communicate efficiently, is one of the most celebrated facets of Apex Legends: Basically, it's a way of annotating the game's virtual world by flagging important features of it with icons that are visible only to your teammates. This system is so comprehensive, in fact, that many players choose to turn off voice chat (though we don't necessarily recommend this).

You should ping your teammates to alert them to both items and situations you want them to know about. Here are some examples:

- Marking loot that you don't need or aren't going to bother to collect, so that your teammates can snag it.
- Pinging to "claim" an item another teammate has marked.
- Pinging an ammo slot in your inventory to request more ammo of that type.
- Pinging an empty weapon slot to let your team know you're in need of a weapon.
- Pinging an empty equipment slot to let your team know you're looking to fill it.
- Marking enemy locations.
- Pinging preset phrases such as "Go," "Enemy," "Looting This Area," "Attacking Here," "Going Here," "Defending This Area," "Watching Here," and "Someone's Been Here."

Use Your Words

Just because the ping system is great doesn't mean you shouldn't use any other method of communication. Ongoing verbal contact with your teammates can, and should, add important information to your pings. For example, it's one thing to mark an enemy, but it is another to verbally add that the enemy is heading west toward a hot-air balloon. Don't hesitate to speak up to add extra information to your pings; at the same time, be careful not to get too chatty. You don't want to distract from the business at hand.

Communicate During the Drop

Every drop has a Jumpmaster, but (as discussed in the drop section) you can free-look to gain information on what other teams are up to. You can also use the ping system to suggest landing locations, and verbal communication to change a drop strategy on the fly. Keep those lines of communication open!

> Down but Not Out

So you're down and bleeding out. Don't give up yet! While you wait to be revived, you can still be be helpful to your team. A few ways you can still pitch in are:

- Pinging points of interest for your teammates.
- Crawling to doorways and blocking them to trap enemy players in buildings.
- Opening and closing doors.
- Keeping an eye out for Wraith's dimensional rifts so you can crawl through to a safer location for teammates to revive you.
- Crawling toward a teammate behind cover to make reviving you safer for them.

> Respawning

The first time you're downed, it takes 90 seconds for your character to bleed out. The second time, it takes 60 seconds. If your teammates are unable to revive you, they'll need to bring you back to a respawn beacon (indicated as a green dot on the map). As long as a teammate is still alive and carrying your banner, that teammate can bring you back to life. Respawning involves collecting a player's banner so make sure you take it! If no banner, no reviving, that's the game.

 Note: Respawned players come back without any equipment, so if you're the reviver rather than the revivee, try to pick a location for your teammate's return to the game that will help them hit the ground running—i.e., a location there's some loot they can snag immediately.

> Only Fools Rush in to Revive a Teammate

The first time a squad member goes down, you have 90 seconds to revive them. Use this time to your advantage and figure out the safest way to get them back on their feet. For example, if a player goes down outside the shrinking circle, it might be smarter to escape inside it to safety, then return once you have recovered health. That said, if you have Wraith on your team, you can use her ultimate ability to open a dimensional rift, and let the downed player crawl through to where you're waiting without taking any damage.

> You Can Mute Squad Mates

If you find yourself matched to teammates who—how should we put this—don't know how to use their indoor voices, you can adjust the volume, or mute them altogether. While we don't recommend turning your back on verbal communication under normal circumstances, sometimes it's better to let the pings do the heavy lifting and give your ears a break.

> Keep Lifeline Safe

If you are playing on a squad that includes Lifeline, keep her safe at all costs. Lifeline's healing and support abilities benefit the whole team, which makes her a priority recipient of good defensive equipment. If you come across the item Ultimate Accelerant, pass this over to Lifeline as well: She'll be able to more frequently use her ultimate ability to summon a care package containing valuable goodies.

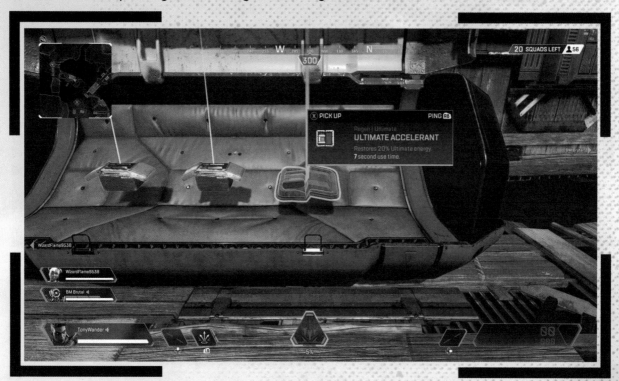

> Share Your Loot

If you've had a good run of finding high-tier loot, consider dropping some of it for teammates, especially if it is gold-tier loot that might work better with another player's chosen legendary character. No matter how powerful your gear is, it will never be as powerful as a well-equipped team that has your back.

> Donate Weapons to Respawned Players

Sure, you worked hard to amass your perfect loadout, but think of how a revived player starts over again with absolutely nothing. Consider donating a weapon to your needy teammate so they can defend themselves, and survive a while, and perhaps someday pay back the favor by reviving you. Remember, you're all in this together, and you're a much more formidable opponent with your teammates than without them.

> Think Ahead - Where to Next?

Before they land, squads should have a rough idea of the path they want to follow through the map. You don't have to stick to this plan religiously, of course, since targets of opportunity will come up, and randomly occurring supply drops and hot zones will occupy your focus, but try to prevent teammates from arguing about where to go next. Don't waste any time because every second counts in Apex Legends.

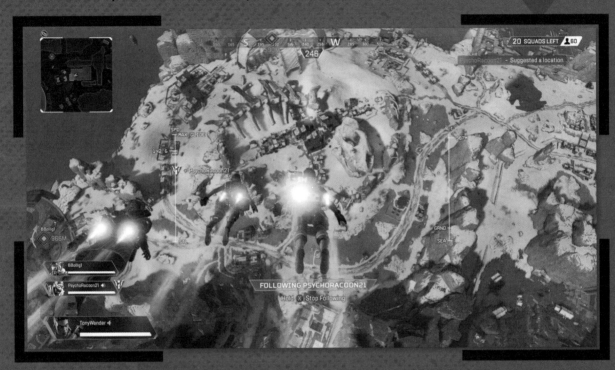

> Flank You Very Much

A common team strategy is to "flank," which means sending a player (or two) around, behind, or to the side of another team while you're engaged in battle. Tactically, it's always better to attack the enemy from multiple directions at once, so if you have fast-moving players like Wraith, Octane, or Pathfinder, always be looking for an opportunity to flank.

> Don't Hesitate to Report a Toxic Player

The player-reporting system is mainly used to identify cheaters and hackers, but don't be afraid to use it to report racist, sexist, or otherwise toxic players. These people ruin the game for you and everyone else, and whenever you choose not to report them, they just go on to bother someone else. Do your part to keep the community of Apex Legends a positive and fun place.

ADVANCED TIPS

If you've been reading carefully, you have more than enough information by now to take your Apex game to the next level. But this section offers some advanced tips, including some basic strategies for early game, mid-game, and endgame.

> Early Game

In the first few minutes of the match, your team should be focused on looting quickly and efficiently. Avoid direct conflict whenever possible, unless you all decide to make a run at a high-tier loot location, like the supply ship.

Have a basic idea of where to go next once you've exhausted your first loot location. Don't be afraid to take down targets of opportunity or get involved in a skirmish, but don't seek out conflict, either. At this stage of the game, the other teams have barely begun expending ammo, healing items, or their character abilities yet. You don't want to be using up precious resources—and making yourself a weaker opponent—so soon.

If you have Pathfinder on your team, try to use his tactical ability to gather information about the circle, as this will help you to choose the next location you and your team can plunder.

Share loot, with the goal of getting every member of your team to a good place, equipment-wise. The sooner everyone is in good fighting condition, the sooner you can aggressively enter the mid-game with confidence.

> Mid-Game

Try to jump into skirmishes between two other weakened teams who have already inflicted damage on each other, so that you can pick them off without great risk to your own and safety.

Continue to loot, potentially targeting more competitive areas like the hot zone or supply ship to snag higher-tier equipment.

Watch the closing circle, and stick to its edges as it contracts. This will give you natural cover at your back, and allow you to catch teams in an ambush if they get stuck outside the circle and have to focus on running to safety rather than watching out for enemies.

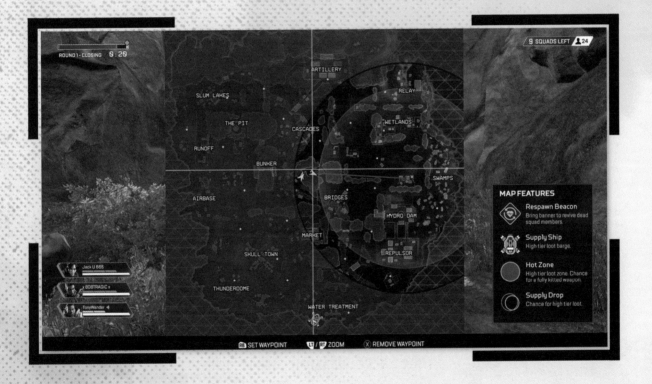

> Endgame

At this stage of the game, finding a position you can defend close to the edge of the circle should be a priority, so always seek out landscape features that will provide strategic advantages to your team.

Many endgames wind up indoors. It can be easier to defend a position that's inside a building, where there are choke points and opportunities for close-quarters combat. Indoors is the ideal location for legendary characters who excel at close-quarters combat, like Caustic, Bloodhound, and Bangalore.

But whenever possible, steer clear of fighting. Teams will be going for the throat as the playing area shrinks, and the longer you can stay out of the fray, the stronger you'll be going into the final battle. If there are three teams left, you want to be the team on the sidelines that's waiting to mop the floor with the weakened victor.

> Launch Pad Boost

Octane's launch-pad ultimate ability sends players soaring high into the air, but if you time a jump just as you bounce off of it, you'll gain a little extra distance.

> Stick to the Edges of Gibraltar's Dome

While enemies can't shoot through Gibraltar's protective dome, you and his other teammate can't shoot out either. Stick near the edges and pop in and out to take on enemies, then retreat to safety. You're useless to the team if you stay near the middle.

> Switch Weapons Instead of Reload

Switching out your weapon is actually quicker than reloading, so when you're in a frantic fight, consider this tactic to gain a little extra advantage. Much better to switch from an empty shotgun to a fully-loaded SMG than to take the time to reload the shotgun.

> Damage Interrupts Finishers

If you see an enemy going for a finisher on a teammate, know that causing them damage can interrupt the whole process. In some cases, rather than defend your downed teammate, you might want to wait for the finisher animation to start, then run in and spoil the enemy's day. This strategy is especially effective with players that can perform a speed boost, like Octane.

Of course, the enemy can interrupt you while you're performing your own finisher, so make sure the coast is clear before you start doing one.

> Damage Does Not Interrupt Revives

Note that damage does not interrupt revives, which means you can choose to take some hits while waiting for your teammate to be returned to full health. That said, if things are too hairy, you can also quit mid-animation and your teammate will still be revived—just with much lower health.

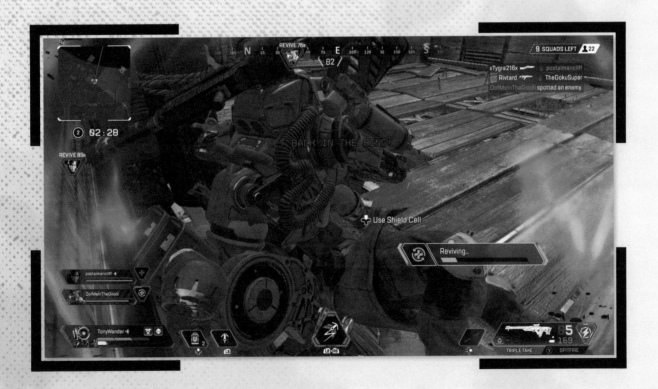

> Change Damage Indicators to "Floating" Rather than "Stacked"

The default damage indicator setting in Apex Legends is "stacked," which means you'll see a combined number reflecting all damage dealt during an attack. Consider changing this to "floating," which shows the specific amount of damage for each damage event. This is more useful, as you can get a feel for how much damage the specific weapons in the game dish out.

> Bunny Hop

This is a technique that involves jumping repeatedly while you're in the midst of a slide. Bunny hopping is slower than sprinting and looks goofy, just like the name suggests, but it's a good move if you're healing, because it makes you a more elusive target for enemy fire.

> The Circle is Your Friend

Get out of the mentality of fearing the circle. Advanced players know that this environmental hazard can be used for their own benefit. A few ways you can exploit the closing circle to your advantage:

• Get between opponents fleeing the shrinking circle and the safe zone. You can hunker down and they will be forced to come to you. The alternative for them is a slow death outside the circle.

• Staying near the inside edge of the circle and rotating around it in a clockwise or counter clockwise direction is a great way to reduce chances of an attack from behind. This strategy is more useful when the circle is smaller.

• Dipping into the circle can be a great way to surprise an enemy who isn't expecting an attack from that direction. If your team is engaged in a battle and you have the speed and healing items to survive a trip outside the circle, you can flank them from the place they least expect. Thanks, circle!

• If there is some valuable loot just outside the circle, it may be worth your time to venture out and get it. You definitely won't have to worry about an ambush, as other teams will have made it a priority to not be there anymore. With a fast legendary character, it might be worth sacrificing a bit of health for a gold-tier piece of equipment.

> Earn Additional XP by Killing the Champion

XP, or experience points, are useful for buying cosmetic items in the Apex Store, so be aware you get a 500 XP bonus for killing the "champion," who's identified at the beginning of every match. The champion is the player with the highest personal-best score in a previous game.

> Grenades Aren't Just for Killing

Grenades are often overlooked as a tool in Apex Legends, as they are hard to aim and the explosion delay is pretty tricky to time in the middle of a fast-paced battle. But consider using grenades to "herd" your enemies into areas that provide combat advantages to you—cover, high ground, etc. A grenade will do some very effective damage if you've managed to force another team into a choke point. A well-timed explosion can also deter an enemy's attempts to push closer to your team.

> You Can Move Death Boxes

You can (clumsily) move around an opponent's death crate by sliding or walking into it. This can be useful in situations where the death crate is near a piece of cover and you want a peaceful looting experience. Wouldn't that be nice?

> The Ring: The Details

The closing ring of death kills you softly, a little bit at a time. Wondering about its specific mechanics? If you aren't, you should be! Respawn Entertainment issued a deep dive into this question for the release of Season 2 of Apex Legends.

Officially, ring damage occurs at the following rates:

- Round 1: 2% damage taken per tick
- Round 2: 5% damage taken per tick
- Round 3: 10% damage taken per tick
- Round 4: 20% damage taken per tick
- Round 5: 20% damage taken per tick
- Round 6 and beyond: 25% damage taken per tick

The closing of the ring now occurs according to the following rules:

First Circle
Starts closing after: 3 minutes
Time to close: 2 minutes
(Note: Ring radius for the first circle has been reduced by roughly 9%)

Second Circle
Starts closing after: 2 minutes 30 seconds
Time to close: 2 minutes

Third Circle
Starts closing after: 2 minutes 15 seconds
Time to close: 2 minutes

Fourth Circle
Starts closing after: 2 minutes
Time to close: 2 minutes

Fifth Circle
Starts closing after: 1 minute 30 seconds
Time to close: 1 minute 40 seconds

Sixth Circle
Starts closing after: 1 minute 30 seconds
Time to close: 1 minute 40 seconds

Seventh Circle
Starts closing after: 2 minutes
Time to close: 1 minute 20 seconds

Eighth Circle
Starts closing after: 20 seconds
Time to close: 1 minute 20 seconds

> Challenges

New for Season 2 of Apex Legends, challenges are the opportunity to earn XP and rewards for completing secondary tasks.

Challenges encourage players to explore more of the game and switch up their play styles. For example, a challenge could involve placing in the top 5 while playing as a specific legendary character, or perhaps racking up a certain amount of kills with a specific weapon. For advanced players, these challenges offer a fun opportunity to approach the game in a different way, and provide an interesting secondary objective to Apex Legends matches aside from Kill or Be Killed (not that there's anything wrong with that).

>*Review Your Performance with Statistics Feature*

As of the update for Season 2, players can now access detailed statistics for their accounts, including:

- How many games you've played.

- How many wins you've racked up.

- How many times your teams have placed in the top 5.

- How much damage you've dealt to other players.

- How many kills you've accumulated.

- Kill/death ratio (the amount of players you've killed divided by the amount of times you've died.)

You can access this information by selecting your name in the lobby.

Respawn has indicated that they will be adding more data to the statistics page, so if there is a stat you'd like to see, write to them and it might appear in the next update!

You can access this information by selecting your name in the lobby.

Respawn has indicated that they will be adding more data to the statistics page, so if there is a stat you'd like to see, write to them and it might appear in the next update!

MICRO TRANSACTIONS

Yes, Apex Legends has an online store, as well as three types of in-game currency! But don't worry, no one can buy his way to victory. Rest assured that nothing you can acquire in the store can improve your combat prowess (unless you consider a flashy new skin a psychological advantage).

THE THREE CURRENCIES

> Crafting Metals

You can only get your mitts on this currency from Apex packs, which you can earn from in-game experience. You can't buy crafting metals with real-world money, and it is used to buy legendary skins but you can buy Apex Packs with real world money to get them directly.

> Legend Tokens

This currency can only be earned by leveling up your account—in other words, simply by playing the game. You can use it to unlock new Legends, such as Octane; it's the only currency that you can use to buy certain exclusive skins.

> Apex Coins

You can purchase Apex coins—which allow you to unlock legendary characters, Apex packs, and featured in-store items—using real-world money. The minimum purchase is 1,000 Apex coins, and it'll set you back $9,99 US ($12,99 CA and 9,99 euros). To give you an idea of purchasing power, unlocking a legendary character costs 750 Apex coins. For players who buy larger quantities at one time, purchase bonuses of extra Apex coins are available.

WHAT YOU CAN BUY

> Battle Pass

You have the option of squeezing more value out of Apex Legends by purchasing a Battle Pass. The Battle Pass allows players to complete challenges, earn exclusive rewards, and access more cosmetic items. It comes in two flavors:

- **Battle Pass**
  The regular Battle Pass, at the price of 950 Apex coins.

- **Battle Pass Bundle**
  Think of this as Battle Pass: Special Edition. Among its extra features: Players gain access to a new skin for the legendary character Caustic, and they have the ability to instantly unlock their next 25 levels for Season 2 instantly. All this, for the price of 2,800 Apex coins.

> Cosmetic Items

As mentioned earlier, none of the items you can buy in the Apex Store will confer a specific in-game advantage (although unlocking legendary characters will obviously give you greater flexibility when joining a squad). So what can you buy there?

- Weapon skins
- Legend skins
- Legend finishers
- Banner frames
- Banner poses

- Banner stat trackers
- Intro quips
- Kill quips
- Crafting metals
- New loading screens

- Drop and victory music
- "Emotes" (physical gestures like a thumbs-up—that your characters use to communicate)

> Featured Items

Featured items include cosmetic items listed above. Note that each item has an expiration date, after which it's removed from the featured section. But items may rotate back into the store, so if you regret missing out on an item, keep checking in. You can also craft some of the featured items with crafting metals

> Unlock Legends

As of Season 1, three Legends are locked: Caustic, Mirage, and Octane. Fortunately, none of these characters top our list of most useful legendary characters, so you're pretty safe to wait until you've played the game long enough to unlock them naturally.

> Apex Packs

Basically a loot box. You naturally earn Apex Packs for free by playing the game and progressing from experience level 1 to 100. You can earn up to 45 free Apex Packs this way.

You can acquire additional Apex Packs from the Apex store. Each one costs 100 Apex Coins and contains three random cosmetic items. Each Apex Pack is guaranteed to include at least one item of rare or better quality, with a 24.8% chance of an item of Epic or better quality, and a 7.4% chance of a Legendary item.

You don't have to worry about receiving a duplicate of an item you've got already: The game keeps track of what you own. You can also bank on getting a guaranteed Legendary item after a maximum of 30 Apex Packs.

HAPPY GAMING!

We hope you found this guide useful, and we're confident that if you practice the strategies outlined here, you will rapidly improve at this fun and competitive battle royale. As Apex Legends is still a relatively new game with a rapidly growing fan base, putting in some time now will earn you many victories in the seasons and years to come. Have fun out there!

 Did you know that an Apex Legends solo mode featuring Octane has been tested? Will it be integrated into the next season? Keep a close eye on it and go check the Apex Legends updates!
https://www.ea.com/games/apex-legends